7012437Z

It couldn't happen—
BUT IT DID!

On a bright, clear winter afternoon, the nine children in the town of Clayton who traveled each day to the Regional School in Lakeview disappeared from the face of the earth, along with the bus in which they traveled and its driver. They vanished as completely as if they had been sucked up into outer space by some monstrous interplanetary vacuum cleaner.

THE DAY
THE CHILDREN VANISHED

"A veteran and a master"   *—Pittsburgh Press*

"A pro among pros"   *—Ellery Queen*

THE DAY
THE CHILDREN
VANISHED

HUGH PENTECOST

PUBLISHED BY POCKET BOOKS NEW YORK

THE DAY THE CHILDREN VANISHED

POCKET BOOK edition published October, 1976

This novel is an expanded version of the short story "The Day the Children Vanished" by Hugh Pentecost.

This original POCKET BOOK edition is printed from brand-new plates made from newly set, clear, easy-to-read type.
POCKET BOOK editions are published by
POCKET BOOKS,
a division of Simon & Schuster, Inc.,
A GULF+WESTERN COMPANY
630 Fifth Avenue,
New York, N.Y. 10020.
Trademarks registered in the United States
and other countries.

ISBN: 978-1-5011-5239-9
Cover illustration by Howard Koslow.

Printed in the U.S.A.

THE DAY
THE CHILDREN
VANISHED

CHAPTER
ONE

On a bright, clear winter's afternoon the children in the town of Clayton who traveled each day to the regional school in Lakeview disappeared from the face of the earth, along with the bus in which they traveled and its driver. They vanished as completely as if they had been sucked up into outer space by some monstrous interplanetary vacuum cleaner.

Actually, in the time of hysteria which followed the disappearance, that theory was put forward by some distraught citizen of Clayton, and not a few people, completely stumped for an explanation, gave consideration to it.

There was, of course, nothing supernatural or interplanetary about the disappearance of nine children, one adult, and their school bus. It was the result of callous human villainy. But, since there was no possible explanation for it, it assumed all the aspects of black magic for tortured parents and a bewildered citizenry.

Clayton is seven miles from Lakeview. It is a

rapidly growing quarry town. Lakeview, considerably larger and with a long history of planning for growth, recently built a new school. It was agreed between the boards of education of the two towns that the children living at the east end of Clayton should be bused to the Lakeview school, where there was adequate space and teaching staff. This busing of children from Clayton to Lakeview bore no relationship to the controversy across the nation over bussing for purposes of integration. It was simply a temporary expedient for dealing with a problem of lack of space. Two black children were among those who made the trip each day, but they weren't being bussed for racial reasons. At least no one would have said so the day before the children vanished.

Since there were only nine children involved, they didn't use one of the big forty-eight-passenger school buses to transport them. A twelve-passenger station wagon was acquired, properly painted and marked as a school bus, and Jerry Mahoney, a mechanic at the East Clayton Garage, was hired to drive the two trips each day with the children.

Jerry Mahoney was well liked and respected. He had been a mechanic in the Air Force during a tour of duty in Vietnam. He was a wizard with engines. He was engaged to be married to Elizabeth Deering, who worked in the Clayton Bank and was one of the town's choice picks. They were both nice people, and responsible.

The disappearance of the school bus, the children, and Jerry Mahoney took place on a two-mile stretch of road where disappearance was impossible. It was called "the dugway," and it wound along the side of Clayton Lake. Heavy wire guard rails protected the road from the lake for the full two-mile stretch. There was not a gap in the steel wire anywhere. At any rate, coming from Lakeview to Clayton the bus would have been on the other side of the road, and the ground there rose abruptly upward into thousands of acres of mountain woodland, so thickly green that not even a tractor could have made its way up any part of it except for fifty yards of an unused road that led to an abandoned quarry. Even over the old road nothing could have passed without leaving a trail of torn brush and broken saplings.

On the day the children vanished the sun had been bright on a frozen landscape, but along toward four-thirty in the afternoon it was beginning to be low in its winter orbit. At the Clayton end of the dugway was Joe Gorman's diner. It was a popular stop for trucks passing through Clayton on Route 14, heading for northern New England. Joe Gorman specialized in jumbo-sized hamburgers, French fries and fried onion rings, and homemade pies baked by Ethel Gorman, his wife. There had been a flurry of business about three-thirty that afternoon, half a dozen truckers laughing and joking over food and coffee and cigarettes. They had kept Joe Gorman in high gear for about forty minutes. He had been too busy to notice that Jerry Mahoney and the school bus hadn't arrived. Gorman's Diner was the first stop on this end of the dugway for the bus, because one of the children it carried was Peter Gorman, Joe Gorman's twelve-year-old son.

The fact that the bus was twenty-five minutes late didn't particularly concern Joe Gorman, a black-haired Irishman with bright blue eyes. He had learned during a hard working life that there was always a perfectly normal explanation for the unusual or the unexpected. His wife, Ethel, was probably fuming at home, he told himself, imagining some disaster. Women were like that. The kids had either been kept late in school for some reason or Jerry Mahoney had had some trouble with the bus, maybe a flat tire.

About four-thirty Joe Gorman began to feel a tingling of concern about the failure of the bus to appear. He put a damper on that when he realized the bus might have come and gone without his noticing it. Peter always came into the diner for an ice cream or a doughnut and milk, but the truckers had been there and Peter might have decided to walk straight home, only a hundred yards or so down Clayton's main street. Joe thought he could have missed the bus while he'd been in the back room getting fresh hamburgers out of the refrigerator. He put a dime in the pay phone and called his wife. Was Peter there?

"No. I thought he was with you, Joe. What's wrong?"

"Nothing's wrong," Joe said. "I had a lot of customers and I missed seeing the bus. Pete didn't come in. He probably went on to the Dicklers' with Donald and Dorothy. He and Donald have been skate-boarding on the hill out there."

"He should have told you he was going there."

"He's twelve years old," Joe said.

"It's not like him."

"I'll call the Dicklers."

The Dicklers' was the second stop for the bus after the dugway. Joe called. Josephine Dickler had begun to worry about Donald and Dorothy. The bus hadn't arrived there yet. Hadn't it stopped at the diner? Joe explained that he thought he might have missed it, but if it hadn't arrived at the Dicklers' it must not have come through the dugway yet.

"What can have happened?" Josephine Dickler asked, obviously concerned.

"Don't get excited," Joe said. "There'll be a simple answer."

"An accident!"

"No chance," Joe said. "People have been coming and going through the dugway. If there'd been an accident we'd have heard. They probably got held up at school for something or other."

A little tingling of fear began to run along Joe Gorman's spine. He was beginning not to believe his own reassurances. He spent a third dime calling the school in Lakeview and found himself connected with Miss Bromfield, the vice-principal. He told her the bus hadn't come through from Lakeview.

"Yours is the third call I've had, Joe," she said. "Jerry and the children left here promptly on time. He should have reached Clayton long before this. The only thing I can think of is he had a flat tire or something. If there'd been an accident someone would have called the school."

"If some kind of a breakdown happened you'd think Jerry would have called in," Joe said. "He'd know the parents would be worrying."

"If it happened in the dugway there'd be no phone nearby," Miss Bromfield said. "He wouldn't want to leave the children alone."

"So he could have flagged someone down and got them to call for him," Joe said. "People going back and forth all the time."

"I suppose so."

"You'll be getting more calls," Joe said. "Nine

children, seven families. I'll check out along Jerry's route."

Joe Gorman closed up his diner and went out back to his jeep. It was only two miles through the dugway. At least he could satisfy himself that nothing had gone wrong there. If the bus had broken down it had to be in the dugway, because if something had happened at the Lakeview end or the Clayton end dozens of people would know about it.

He drove the jeep briskly through the dugway, glancing from time to time at the steel wire guard rail on the lake side. There was no sign of the bus. The last rays of the afternoon sun didn't penetrate into the dugway and it was like driving through a semi-dark tunnel.

At the Lakeview end was Jake Nugent's gas station and garage. Here there was sunlight. Joe Gorman had known Jake Nugent all his life. The old man was known as a "character" in town. He'd been a blacksmith countless years ago and when the horse ceased to be a means of transportation he'd gone to selling gas to help support an iron-work and welding business. Jake had been old when Joe Gorman was a kid. He must be old as God now, Joe thought.

Jake greeted a potential customer cheerfully.

"Sure I saw Jerry and his bus when they were headed for Clayton," Jake said.

"When was that?"

"Twenty past three," Jake said. "You can tell time by Jerry." He expectorated a stream of tobacco juice that stained his scraggly beard yellow.

"If you tell time by him, maybe he was late and you didn't know it," Joe said.

"Right on the button," Jake said. "He stopped

And it couldn't have gone up the wooded mountain on the other side.

Joe Gorman felt better as he parked his jeep and reopened the diner. He felt better, but he felt a little dizzy from trying to make sense out of the situation. Five minutes later Trooper Samuel Teliski came whizzing through from the Lakeview end.

"What's the gag?" he asked Joe. Sun and wind gave his young face a leathery look.

Joe tried to light a cigarette and found his hands shaking as he attempted to light a match. Teliski snapped on his lighter and held it out. Joe dragged smoke deep into his lungs.

"The bus started through the dugway at the regular time," he said. "Twenty past three. Jake Nugent saw it. Jerry brought him a letter and Jake watched the bus head into the dugway. It never came out this end."

A nerve twitched in Teliski's cheek. "The lake," he said.

Joe shook his head. "I thought of that," he said. "I just came through ahead of you, looking. Not a scratch on a post. It didn't go into the lake; I'll stake my life on that."

"Then what else?" Teliski asked. "It couldn't go up the mountain."

"I know," Joe said.

The two men stared at each other.

"Jake was wrong," Teliski said. "The bus couldn't have gone into the dugway. It must have headed toward Millwood."

"Why? None of the kids live out that way."

"Maybe Jerry had mail for someone else," Teliski said.

"It went into the dugway. Jake is certain. He watched it go."

"So it has to be some kind of a joke," Teliski said.

"What kind of a joke? It's no joke to me, or the Dicklers, or other people who had kids on the bus."

"Maybe they had permission to go to some kind of special movie or something."

Joe shook his head again, stubbornly. "There was nothing special. I spoke to Miss Bromfield at the school. If there'd been anything special the parents would have been notified. Look, Teliski, it doesn't make sense, but the bus went into the dugway and it didn't come out. It's not in the dugway now and it didn't go into the lake."

"And it couldn't climb the mountain," Teliski said. He made an attempt at common sense. "I'll check back on the guard rail, but let's say you're right. The goddamn thing couldn't take wings and fly away. So it didn't go into the dugway."

"That's logic," Joe said. "But why should Jake Nugent lie? Jerry's an hour and three quarters late now. If he didn't go into the dugway, where is he? Where could he go, and why? Why hasn't he telephoned if everything is okay?"

A car pulled up outside the diner and a man came charging in through the door. It was Karl Dickler, father of Donald and Dorothy Dickler, two of the missing kids.

"Thank God you're here, Teliski," he said. "What's happened?"

"Some kind of a gag," Teliski said. "The bus didn't come through the dugway. Jake Nugent thought he saw it start in, but he must have been mistaken. For some reason Jerry must have driven off toward Millwood."

"But it did start through the dugway!" Dickler said. "I passed it myself on the way to Lakeview, about a half mile this way from Jake's place. I saw it. I waved at my own kids!"

"It never came out this end," Joe Gorman said, in a choked voice.

Dickler swayed and reached out to the trooper to steady himself. "Oh, Jesus," he said. "The lake!"

But they were not in the lake. The three men went back through the dugway, creeping slowly along. Joe Gorman's original survey proved to be correct. There was no broken wire, no bent posts, nothing. The bus couldn't have jumped the guard rail. It was a relief to be reassured, but it deepened the mystery.

CHAPTER
TWO

where, somehow, and the only person who could have done it is Jerry Mahoney. The bus had to be driven somewhere—it couldn't navigate by itself. The only person who could have driven it was Jerry."

"Why would he do such a thing?" Warren Jennings asked. He was a neat, well-groomed black man, a crew foreman at the Clayton quarries.

"We have to think it's a mass kidnapping," Dickler said.

"But none of us is rich!" George Isham said. "No one could hope to get any kind of real money from any of us."

"There are seven families involved," Dickler said. "But the whole town could be caught up in this thing. Our friends and neighbors wouldn't let our kids be hurt. He could ask for God knows how much."

"He?" Joe Gorman asked.

"Jerry Mahoney, who else? He managed it, however it was done. He had to be in on it, even if there are others involved. We'll all get ransom letters in the morning. You'll see."

"I've known Jerry ever since he and his old man moved into town ten years ago," Joe Gorman said. "I can't believe he's involved."

"Who else?" Dickler demanded. "It had to be carefully planned in advance. The bus couldn't simply disappear without a whole scheme worked out ahead of time. Jerry had to know and be a part of it."

"It could be his old man and his girl are just as worried about him as we are about our kids," Warren Jennings said.

Dickler looked at Jennings, and you could see he

thought because the man's skin was black he didn't think like other people.

"He was in the war in Vietnam," Dickler said. "A lot of boys who were in the war came back unstable. I know we've thought of Jerry as a decent, hard-working, respectable member of the community. So maybe he's flipped his wig. Our kids are gone and he had to be a part of what happened."

"Maybe he's been gambling. Maybe he needs money to pay off debts to some bookie," Fred Williams said. "Who knows, maybe he needs money to skip town for some reason. I think we should talk to his old man and Liz Deering about him."

"The main thing is to find the kids," Sergeant Mason said. "You could be right, Dickler, but this can't be the way it looks. What we have to do is come up with a sensible explanation. The sooner we do that the sooner we'll get the children back."

"I tell you how you'll find that explanation, Sergeant," Karl Dickler said. "Check into Jerry Mahoney. Find out who his friends are, here in town and out of town. Find out who he owes and how much."

"His girl, Liz Deering, works in the bank," Roger Trent said. "She could tell us about his finances."

"If she would," Dickler said, his voice dark with suspicion.

Warren Jennings shook his head. "You're making a villain out of Mahoney before you have a scrap of evidence against him."

Sergeant Joseph Mason was an experienced officer. He had once worked in a big city and had asked for this rural assignment because of a sick wife. He had seen the beginnings of mass hysteria before. It lay at the root of lynch-mob actions and witch hunts. Unable to find their children or any explanation for their disappearance, these people would focus their attention on Jerry Mahoney and his father and his girl. It could, he knew, make for a bad scene.

"It might be a good idea to talk to Pat Mahoney and Liz Deering," he said. Oppose the notion and he would only fan the flames.

"Well, let's go!" Karl Dickler said.

"Just two or three of us," Mason said.

"Count me in," Dickler said. "Because I'll get the truth out of Pat Mahoney whether I go with you or not. Jerry Mahoney has got my two kids and he's going to pay for it."

"Even if he didn't do anything," Warren Jennings said. He could smell hysteria as well as Sergeant Mason. He had seen burning crosses in his time, and men in white hoods.

"If you aren't interested in saving your own kids that's your business, Jennings!" Karl Dickler shouted at him.

"If Pat Mahoney knows anything that would hurt Jerry, he isn't going to tell us about it," Joe Gorman said.

"We'll make the sonofabitch talk if he knows anything," Dickler said. "Let's go!"

Nobody had thought of Pat Mahoney as a sonofabitch until that moment. Nor was Karl Dickler a bad man. He was in the grip of a fear so devastating he wasn't entirely rational. His two children, Donald and Dorothy, might be gone forever. He'd tried to soothe his wife, Josephine, whose white and stricken face was a mask of terror. Their lives were built around the children. Inaction was intolerable. There was no one else to aim at but Jerry Mahoney, so he took aim.

The Mahoneys, father and son, had come to Clayton ten years ago. If you weren't born and brought up in Clayton you weren't thought of as a "native." You were an "out-of-towner." It was a wartime friendship that brought the Mahoneys to Clayton. Jimmy Craven, a local boy, had served in the Air Force with Jerry Mahoney in Vietnam. Jimmy's father owned and ran the East Clayton Garage. The elder Craven died while his son was still overseas, and Jimmy came back from the war unscathed and ready to take over his inheritance, the garage. He brought Jerry Mahoney with him. Jerry was a first-rate mechanic. He was glad to have a job when he got out of service. People came to like and trust him, and people around the area who owned foreign cars brought them to East Clayton for servicing because Jerry knew all there was to know about engines.

After about six months, when it was apparent that he fitted into Jimmy Craven's picture, Jerry rented a small cottage in town and brought his father to Clayton to live with him.

Pat Mahoney was not like anyone the people of Clayton had known before. He was a spritely little man of seventy with snow-white hair and the brightest blue eyes you ever saw. He was an old-time vaudevillian. Show business had been his whole life. He had married a show girl long ago, a singer and dancer named Nora Faye, and Mahoney & Faye had been a successful vaudeville act for years, with soft-shoe dances and songs and a sprinkling of Pat Mahoney's Irish wit. Nora had died some time before the migration to Clayton, the famous team was broken up forever, and Pat

diamond in a heavy gold setting he wore on his little finger.

"Any news?" he asked Sergeant Mason. Then, as he looked around at the sergeant's little army, his blue eyes stopped twinkling. If there was news he knew it wasn't good.

"All right, Pat," Sergeant Mason said. "What's Jerry done with those kids?"

The girl looked up at the men, her tearstained face shocked. Pat Mahoney's bright blue eyes met the sergeant's stare steadily. Then crinkles of mirth appeared at the corners of his eyes and mouth.

"I'd like to ask you something before I try to answer that, Sergeant," Pat Mahoney said.

"Well?"

"Have you stopped beating your wife, Sergeant?"

Nobody laughed when Pat pulled that old court-room wheeze. Pat looked past the sergeant at Trooper Teliski, Joe Gorman, Mr. and Mrs. Dickler, and Ronald Peabody, the fat and wheezing sheriff.

"That question I asked you, Sergeant," Pat said, "makes just about as much sense as the one you asked me. You asked what Nora's boy has done with those kids. There's no answer to that question, because it isn't sensible. Do I hear you saying, 'I know how you must be feeling, Pat Mahoney, and you, Elizabeth Deering? And is there anything we can do for you in this hour of your terrible anxiety?' I don't hear you saying anything like that, Sergeant."

"I'm sorry, Pat," Mason said. "Those kids are missing. Jerry had to take them somewhere."

"No!" Liz Deering cried out. "You all know Jerry better than that."

She looked into their faces and saw that they

didn't. She supposed they could be forgiven. Even in her own fear for the man she loved she supposed that. You can't confront people with the inexplicable without frightening them and throwing them off balance. You can't endanger their children and expect a sane reaction. They muttered angrily, and she saw the tortured faces of Joe Gorman and Karl Dickler, and the swollen red eyes of Josephine Dickler. She felt sorry for them, in spite of her outrage at their suggestion that Jerry was the villain of the piece.

"Has Jerry talked in any way queerly to you, Pat?" Sergeant Mason asked. "Has he acted normal of late?"

"Nora's boy is the most normal boy you ever met," Pat Mahoney said. "You know that, Sergeant. Why, you've known him for ten years."

Mrs. Dickler screamed out. "He'd protect his son! Naturally he'd protect his son. But Jerry's stolen our children!"

"The Pied Piper rides again," Pat Mahoney said.

"Make him talk!" Josephine Dickler cried, and the others muttered behind her.

"When did you last see Jerry?" Mason asked.

"Breakfast," Pat said. "He has his lunch at Joe Gorman's diner." The corner of his mouth twitched. "He should have been home long ago for dinner."

"Did he eat at your diner at noon, Joe?" Mason asked Gorman.

"Like always," Joe said.

"Seem normal?"

"No different from any other day," Joe admitted.

Mason turned back to Pat Mahoney. "Did he have a need for money?"

"Money? He was a man respected——until now——

wasn't he? He was a man with a fine girl in love with him, wasn't he? What need would he have for money?"

"Make him answer sensibly!" Mrs. Dickler pleaded in a despairing voice.

Joe Gorman stepped forward. "Pat, maybe Jerry got sick all of a sudden. It's happened to men who saw action overseas. Maybe you saw signs of something and wouldn't want to tell of it. But my Pete was on that bus, and Karl's two. We're nowhere, Pat. So if you can tell us anything—? Our kids were on that bus!"

Pat Mahoney's eyes, as he listened to Joe Gorman, filled with pain. "My kid was on that bus, too, Joe," he said.

They all stared at him, the parents with a kind of hatred. And then, in the distance, they heard the wail of a siren. A trooper's car was coming through the dugway, hell-bent.

"Maybe it's news," someone shouted.

"News!"

They all went stumbling out of the house to meet the approaching car—all but Liz Deering, who stayed behind clinging to the old man, who hadn't moved from his chair.

"I don't understand it," she said, her voice shaken. "They think Jerry's harmed their children, Pat! Why? Why would they think he'd do such a thing? *Why*?"

Old Pat's eyes had a faraway look in them. "Did I ever tell you about The Great Thurston?" he asked. "Greatest magic act I ever saw."

"Pat!" Liz said, her eyes widening.

"First time I ever caught his act was in Sioux City," Pat said. "He came out in a flowing cape, a silk hat, and he—" His voice trailed off.

Dear God, he's losing his reason, Liz Deering told herself. Let the news be good before everything falls apart. Let them be found safe.

Outside the siren drew close.

The police car with its wailing siren brought news, but it was not the sort of news the people of Clayton were hoping to hear.

It was reassuring to know that within a few hours of the tragedy the entire area was alerted, that the moment daylight came a fleet of army helicopters would cover the area for hundreds of miles around, that a five-state alarm was out for the missing bus and its passengers, and that the attorney general was sending the best man on his staff to direct and coordinate the search. Somehow, outside help seemed more likely to succeed than the local troopers and their friends and neighbors.

Top officials, viewing the case coldly and untouched by the hysteria of personal involvement, had a theory. Of course there had to be a rational explanation for the disappearance of the bus, and Clyde Haviland, a tall, stoop-shouldered, scholarly-looking investigator from the attorney general's office, was ordered to produce that explanation as soon as possible. But privately, officials had no doubt as to the reason for the disappearance. This was a mass kidnapping, something novel in the annals of crime. Or was it? Had the criminal or criminals learned something from the operations of present-day terrorists who hijacked planes and held innocent people hostage? Since none of the individual families were wealthy, officials were convinced that the next move in this strange charade would be a demand on the whole community to pay ransom for the children. The FBI was alerted and promised all-out help.

Trained help was on the way, but meanwhile it was dark and cold and nine children were out there, helpless, being treated God knows how. It would be seven or eight hours before there'd be enough light for any kind of official search to begin.

And any moment the ransom demands might come. By phone? By a letter shoved under someone's door? There would be no sleep for the parents of the missing children. There would be no sleep for Pat Mahoney and Liz Deering. The night would drag on and on forever.

The state trooper barracks was alert for a call from anyone from anywhere. The missing vehicle and the children could be miles away by now. It had been almost two hours after Jake Nugent saw the bus go into the dugway before any kind of an alarm was issued. Troopers from three states were on the lookout for it already. By now, with the certainty that an alarm was out, the criminal or criminals would surely have abandoned the easily spotted bus, transferred their hostages to another vehicle or vehicles, or made them prisoners in some unpredictable hiding place. When the bus was spotted, they'd at least have a notion in what direction and what area to concentrate a search.

Clyde Haviland arrived in Clayton shortly before midnight. People knew him in Clayton. He had solved a particularly brutal murder in the neighboring town of Johnsville a couple of years back. His work on that case had brought him in and out of Clayton for several weeks, and the people knew that this calm, quiet man had the tenacity of a bulldog. If anyone could solve this mystery, he was their best bet.

Haviland didn't wait for morning to get to work. He set up a headquarters in the town hall, where there was more than one telephone. He listened patiently to the various stories and accounts from Sheriff Peabody, and Mason and Teliski of the local troopers. He talked to only two of the parents —Joe Gorman, who had first searched the dugway, and Karl Dickler, who was the town's second selectman. He wanted facts, not emotions. While mothers wept and menfolk gathered outside the town hall grumbling angrily, Haviland reached out for information. He contacted the Air Force in Washington, D.C., and asked for a complete file on Technical Sergeant Jerry Mahoney. As the night wore on, men who had known Jerry Mahoney in the service were waked from their sleep to be questioned. Had Jerry ever said anything or done anything that would lead them to think he might move into a world of violence? Did his medical history contain any record of mental illness?

The local bank president was asked for a report on Jerry's checking and savings accounts. Around two in the morning the special agent in charge of the local field division of the FBI checked in at the town hall. They had lifted Jerry's fingerprints from his toolbox in the East Clayton Garage and sent them to Washington. The FBI man's name was Frank Parker.

He reacted to the story as everyone else did when they first heard it.

"Of course the bus never went into the dugway," he said.

Then he heard that Jake Nugent had seen it go in, and that Karl Dickler had actually passed it in the dugway, waving at his children.

"So it had to come out the Clayton end," Parker said. "But how could nobody see it? At least no one remembers seeing it. It was an everyday event. This Mahoney could have driven straight through town with nobody paying attention. Like the post-man."

"What postman?" Sergeant Mason asked.

"Old detective story gimmick," Parker said. "People say no one went into a building. But the postman did, and nobody saw him because he was an everyday event. People say nobody went in be-cause the postman was nobody. He was routine."

"I just don't buy that," Joe Gorman said.

Parker gave him a wry smile. "I don't either, but I thought I'd mention it. He could have turned around and gone back to Lakeview, couldn't he?"

"He'd have been seen there," Haviland said quietly. "He wasn't supposed to be in Lakeview, so he wouldn't be like the postman there."

"It's going down toward zero outside," Ronald Peabody, the sheriff, said glumly. "If those kids are outdoors somewhere—"

"They're one hell of a long way from here by now if you ask me," Sergeant Mason said.

Haviland looked at him, his eyes unblinking behind the lenses of his schoolteacher glasses. "Except that they never came out of the dugway," he said.

"Nobody saw them," Mason said. "But they're not in the dugway, so they did come out. Some way."

"Maybe someone reached down out of the heavens and snatched that school bus up into space," Haviland said. He looked around at serious, startled faces, and something he saw made him add quickly: "I'm kidding, of course."

Peabody laughed nervously. "It's the only good explanation we've had so far," he said.

About five o'clock in the morning, still two hours to enough daylight for an outdoor search to begin, Haviland's telephones began to ring. He answered, speaking in monosyllables, saying thanks to each caller. Finally he leaned back in his chair, polishing his shell-rimmed glasses with a white linen handkerchief.

"So far," he said with a faint smile, "the report on Jerry Mahoney is quite extraordinary."

"In what way?" Sergeant Mason asked, eager for the scent of blood.

"Model citizen," Haviland said. "No one has a bad word for him. No bad temper. Never held grudges. Never chiseled anyone. Saves his money. After all, he was going to get married. His savings account in the local bank would surprise some of you. On the face of it, he is the last person in the world to suspect."

"There has to be a first time for everything," Karl Dickler said. He put his hand up to his cheek. There was a nerve there that had started to twitch, regularly as the tick of a clock. "I always liked Jerry Mahoney. Yesterday I'd have given the same kind of report on him you've been getting, Mr. Haviland. But you can't pass up the facts. I'd have said he'd defend those kids with his life—yesterday. But did he? And the old man, his father—he won't answer questions directly. There's something queer about him. Damn it, Mr. Haviland, my kids are out there somewhere." He waved toward the frost-coated window panes.

"Every highway within two hundred miles of here is being patrolled, Mr. Dickler," Haviland said. "If they'd driven straight through the dugway, straight through Clayton, Parker's postman theory might hold up. But once they were five miles away from Clayton, off their regular route, they'd have been noticed. A bright yellow vehicle, painted with school-bus markings, someplace where it ought not to be? There isn't one report of anyone seeing that bus anywhere. Oh, they might not have reported it at the time they saw it, but by now the alarm is out; it's been on the radio and television. They'd remember having seen it, wouldn't they? There hasn't been one report." Haviland paused to light a cigarette. His tapering fingers were nicotine-stained.

"If you'd ever investigated a crime, Mr. Dickler, you'd know we're always swamped with calls from people who think they've seen the wanted man. Here we've got a bus. A busload of kids. Somebody *had* to see it. But there hasn't been a single crackpot call. If there was someplace Mahoney could have stayed under cover in the dugway—and don't tell me, I know there isn't—and started moving after dark, he might get some distance without being noticed. But after dark the alarms were out. He couldn't have traveled five miles then without being trapped."

"We've told ourselves all these things for hours," Dickler said, pinching savagely at his twitching cheek. "What are you going to do, Haviland?"

"Unless we're all wrong we're going to hear from the kidnappers soon," Clyde Haviland said. "Tonight, or in the morning, by mail, or phone, or some unexpected way. But we'll hear. They'll demand money. What other purpose can there be in all this? Once we hear we'll have to start to play it by ear. That's the way these cases are."

"Meanwhile, you just sit here and wait!" Dickler said, a kind of despair in his voice. "What am I going to say to my wife?"

"I think all the parents of the children should go home," Haviland said. "You may be the one the kidnappers contact. It may be your child they put on the phone to convince you the kids are safe. As soon as it's daylight—"

"You think the kids *are* safe?" Dickler cried out.

Haviland stared at the distraught father for a moment, and then he spoke gently. "What kind of assurance can I give you, Mr. Dickler? Even if I tried, you wouldn't believe me. People who play this kind of game are without feelings, they aren't rational. When you fight them you have to walk quietly. If you scare them God knows what you can expect. That's why I ask you all to go home and wait." He dropped his cigarette on the floor and heeled it out. "And pray," he added.

And so it was that the parents of the missing children went home, not to sleep certainly, perhaps to pray. "To sweat it out," Joe Gorman said as he left Haviland's headquarters. The whole town, most of the people awake even if their own children were safe, had visions of the missing kids huddled somewhere in the bitter cold without anything to eat or anything hot to drink. They had joined a world-wide brotherhood, the victims of terrorists. In some quarters there was the futile talk of vengeance against whoever was responsible. Lynch-mob anger was simmering in the quiet town of Clayton.

About six o'clock in the morning Haviland was sipping at a carton of hot coffee when Jimmy Craven, the owner of the East Clayton Garage, barged into the office. Jimmy was the man who had brought Jerry Mahoney to Clayton and taken him into his business. He was a slim, dark-haired, athletic young man, his face leathered by sun and winter winds.

"You're Haviland?"

"Yes," Clyde Haviland said.

"What the hell is all this crazy talk about Jerry Mahoney?"

"It would help if I knew who you are," Haviland said.

"I'm Jerry's friend, his employer—James Craven. I own the East Clayton Garage."

"Well, Mr. Craven, where have you been? We've been trying to locate you most of the night."

"I took a couple of days off to go skiing up in Vermont," Craven said. "Somebody heard what had happened here on the radio, and woke me out of a sound sleep. I've been driving for the last three hours. On the car radio I heard Jerry was the chief suspect. That's crap!"

"It's hard to imagine the bus disappearing without cooperation from its driver," Haviland said.

"It's harder to imagine him cooperating—if you knew him," Craven said. "I stopped at Gorman's Diner on the way in. There's crazy talk there. I swear, they're threatening to string Jerry up when they find him. He's guilty without a chance to speak a word for himself."

"Nobody's going to string him up," Haviland said. "But tell me, since you know him so well, have you had any reason recently to think he was in any sort of trouble? Money trouble is what I have in mind."

"Jerry?" Craven laughed. "He's been squeezing every nickel he's got. He's getting married, you know."

"I know. Was he a betting man? Could he be in trouble with a bookmaker somewhere?"

"Not Jerry. He's the most level-headed guy I know. If he needed money he could walk into the Clayton Bank and float a loan. He's solid in this town."

"He *was* solid," Haviland said. "What could persuade him to drive those kids away somewhere?"

"A gun at his head," Craven said.

"How would he act in a tight corner like that?" Haviland asked.

"Tight corner?" Craven seemed to turn inward toward some memory he was reluctant to face. "Oh, Jerry had himself in one of the tightest corners I can think of in Vietnam, and I'll never forget what he did. That's when I made certain I'd always have him for a friend." Craven's eyes widened. "Funny thing, but that involved kids, too."

Haviland sat quite still.

"I guess you'd call it a search-and-destroy operation," Craven said. "A copter had gone down near some village north of Saigon with twenty paratroopers aboard. Men didn't have a chance to jump, but the pilot landed without anyone being more than shook up. According to one report, a group of villagers armed with the most modern Chinese rapid-fire weapons came out of the woods and mowed down all but one of them—pilot, copilot, and nineteen paratroopers. The killers were almost certainly Viet Cong, but they didn't wear uniforms and the soldier who got away called them 'villagers.'

"Well, Jerry and I were both in the company sent out to search for the killers and mop up after them. Commanding the unit was a Lieutenant Boyd. He wasn't an officer we loved or wanted to follow into any kind of hot spot. We'd seen him in action before. He liked to kill. He enjoyed killing." Craven moistened his lips. "There were a lot of people like Boyd out there. They had a contempt for the Vietnamese, friend or foe—they had yellow skins, for Christ's sake! Boyd was the kind of man the brass would put in charge. He wouldn't hesitate to wipe out anyone who got in his way. Men like me and Jerry and a lot of the rest might hesitate to make sure we didn't gun down an innocent farmer. Boyd wouldn't ask questions. He'd just wipe out anyone he saw, taking it for granted that the villagers had hidden the Viet Cong, collaborated with them." Craven paused to light a cigarette. His hands weren't quite steady. Haviland sat silent, his eyes unblinking.

"We went in, three truckloads of us," Craven said. "We began by tossing some mortar shells and incendiary grenades into the village—just a bunch of thatched huts and cottages. Everything started to burn and the people—the people started to run in all directions. I can still see Boyd, armed with a machine pistol, mowing them down, shooting them in the back. He was like a crazy man, screaming curses as he killed. And then—then we saw the children. There were a couple of dozen or more, all crowded together. I remember thinking they must have been at school when we attacked. Two women were trying to herd them to safety. I saw Boyd open up on the kids, saw one of the women cut in half. Little kids! They couldn't have collaborated with anyone.

"Then I saw Jerry Mahoney—Sergeant Mahoney he was then, second in command. He ran up to Boyd and yanked the machine pistol out of his hands. We couldn't hear what they said, but Boyd was yelling and his face was all twisted up in rage. Then Boyd grabbed the pistol back and aimed it at Jerry. Thank God for quick-witted Mahoney—he knocked the lieutenant flat on his can and took away the gun again. By then most of the kids had gotten to cover. I guess everyone but Boyd had been firing over their heads.

"I knew—we all knew—Jerry would face a court martial, maybe get a firing squad for what he'd done. Boyd would never let him go. Jerry knew that too, but it hadn't stopped him."

"Took guts," Haviland said.

"That's Jerry. He'd never hesitate to do the right thing, no matter what the rules were. He couldn't watch those kids get killed."

"Was he courtmartialed?"

Craven looked away. "Boyd never came out of it. Sniper's bullet—they said."

"Who said?" Haviland asked.

"It could have been a sniper's bullet," Craven said quietly.

Haviland waited a moment. "So you think Jerry Mahoney wouldn't have been panicked by armed kidnappers? How would he have reacted?"

"Cool," Craven said. "He wouldn't do something crazy with those kids to protect. He'd wait for his chance. I tell you, Mr. Haviland, I'd rather have Jerry on my side if I was in trouble than anyone I know. He isn't thinking about himself at this moment. He's thinking about those kids."

Haviland nodded. "That's the general picture I have of him from other sources."

"What can I do to help?" Craven asked.

"Come up with an explanation of how they went into the dugway and never came out," Haviland said. "It's got us all stumped. Seriously, do what you can to calm people down."

The phone on Haviland's desk rang and he picked it up.

"Mr. Haviland?" The voice was hoarse, shaken. "This is Warren Jennings." The black man whose two children were on the bus.

"There's no news, Mr. Jennings," Haviland said. Calls were coming from parents every fifteen or twenty minutes.

"I—I've heard from them," Jennings said.

"Heard from who?"

"The kidnappers," Jennings said. "We—we're supposed to raise five hundred thousand dollars." There was a cackling, despairing laugh. "A half a million bucks. When it's raised they'll tell us where to take it."

Haviland's hand tightened on the phone receiver. "Get down here as quickly as you can, Mr. Jennings."

"There's no way to raise that kind of money," Jennings said in a broken voice.

"Get down here in a hurry," Haviland repeated.

CHAPTER FOUR

The news spread like a forest fire in a drought. Long before Jennings reached Haviland's office people were running through the gray dawn light from house to house. "The kidnappers have made contact! They're asking for a half million dollars— a million dollars!" Jennings's car was surrounded by men and women as he pulled up outside the town clerk's office.

"What did they say?"

"How much did they want?"

"Are the kids all right?"

"Where did they call from?"

"Was it Jerry Mahoney who called?"

Trooper Teliski, who had been snatching a little shut-eye in a back office, was on hand to help Jennings get through the anxious crowd and into the office where Haviland, Sergeant Mason, and Sheriff Peabody were waiting. Haviland had already sent for the president of the Clayton Bank and the town selectmen. He didn't need to be told that the seven families whose children were miss-

ing couldn't begin to raise the amount Jennings
had mentioned on the phone. He had been certain
from the beginning that when the time for ransom
came it would be so much money that it would in-
volve the whole community.

Jennings kept moistening his lips, as though his
mouth were bone dry.

"Let's have it, right from the top," Haviland said.

Jennings sank down in a chair beside the special
investigator's desk. He appeared to be in a state of
exhaustion.

"I—I didn't go to bed," he said. "I thought—
thought there'd be some news from somewhere. I
sat down in an armchair by the telephone, and I
must have dozed off because the ringing woke me
up." He licked his lips again. "I picked up the phone
and just said hello, thinking it might be you, Mr.
Haviland, or one of the other parents. The phone
brought my wife in from the next room. I guess she
was sleeping pretty light, too—if at all."

"Get to it, man," Sergeant Mason said.

"Let him tell it his own way," Haviland said,
quietly. "You know exactly what time it was, Mr.
Jennings?"

"Just before I called you," he said. "Maybe ten
minutes past six."

"Go on."

"I said hello, and this kind of muffled voice
asked if I was Mr. Jennings. I said I was. I
thought it was another newspaper man."

"Another?"

Jennings shook his head from side to side. "Reporters from all over have been calling all night. I
guess the others must have had calls, too."

"A dozen of them," Karl Dickler said. He had just

walked in the door, unshaven, red-eyed. "Did you recognize the voice, Warren? Was it Jerry Mahoney?"

Jennings wasn't sure. "It sounded muffled, like he was holding a handkerchief or something over the mouthpiece. It could have been anyone."

"But it was a man?" Haviland asked.

"I'm sure of that," Jennings said.

"So what did he say, for Christ's sake?" Mason demanded.

"You want your kids back, raise five hundred thousand dollars in twenties and tens, unmarked. That's all he said at first. I told him there was no way we could raise that kind of money, man. You'll raise it if you want to see your kids again, he said. How do we know the kids are all right, I asked him. You got to believe, he said. You got to believe, Mr. Jennings. Then he said he'd call back later in the day, after we'd had a chance to get the money together, to tell us how to deliver it. I said, if we could get the money together we'd have to know the kids were okay before we handed it over. And he said it again: 'You got to believe.' And then he hung up before I could say anything more to him."

Parker, the FBI man, had come in while Jennings was talking. "Right out of the book," he said. "Muffled voice, the whole bag. They've seen it on television a thousand times."

"What do we do?" Jennings asked. He sounded defeated. "No way to raise that kind of money. Oh, God!" He covered his face with his hands.

"We can have Jennings's phone tapped so when they call back—" Sheriff Peabody began.

"Waste of time," Parker said. "They won't call Jennings again. They'll know we'd be ready for them if they did. They'll call somebody else—one of the other parents, or Haviland, or you, or the troopers. They won't talk long enough for you to trace a call. They're not dummies."

"You keep saying 'they,'" Dickler said. "I'm still betting on Jerry Mahoney. He knows who to call, he knows all the kids and their parents. He knows this countryside like the back of his hand. He hunts the woods here every fall. He'll know a safe place to drop off the money."

"What money?" Jennings said in a stifled voice. "I might raise a thousand dollars cash. How about you, Dickler?"

The nerve in Dickler's face was twitching again. "Maybe five," he said, "by increasing the mortgage on my house."

"We'd be lucky to raise twenty thousand among us," Jennings said. "Would they—would they take less than they're asking, knowing there's no way we can put together what they want?"

"They don't expect you to raise it," Haviland said in his quiet voice. "They expect the whole town to raise it."

"The town? Why would anyone else but the parents put up money?" Jennings asked.

"I imagine there are plenty of people in this town wouldn't want the slaughter of those kids on their consciences," the FBI man said. "That's the way they're figuring it, anyway."

"Oh, Jesus!" Dickler said. "You think they'd—?"

"They want you to think they will," Haviland said. "We have some time. Helicopters will be in the air in another hour. The bank won't open for another two hours. The only place you could get a half a million dollars in tens and twenties is at the bank, and they wouldn't have it on hand. They'd have to get it somewhere, from neighboring banks. I'm guessing there won't be another call till noon or later. That gives us time."

"For what?" Dickler asked.

"To figure out how to raise the money," Haviland said. "To decide what we're going to do when we have raised it. Parker's right, you know. They've seen it all on television. When they call they'll tell you one person, acting alone, will leave the money somewhere. They'll tell you 'No cops, no stake-out. Or else.'"

"I forgot something," Jennings said. He raised his heavy black eyelids. "If the money is marked, forget about the kids, he said."

"We can mark it so they'll never know it," Parker said. "We'll have the serial number of every bill. Every cashier and counter man within a thousand miles will be looking for tens and twenties, marked our way, with our numbers on them."

"No!" Karl Dickler shouted. "If we can raise the money somehow, we don't screw things up by going against them. Those are our kids, Parker."

Haviland seemed to be through listening. "I want all the parents to be at home," he said. "There'll be a call, and it could go to any one of them. Don't try to stall them when the call comes. Get your instructions. Agree to whatever they say. But try to insist on one thing. You've got to talk to one of the kids to be sure they're all right. They may tell you the kids aren't where they're calling from. Insist they get one or more of the kids to a phone and call again."

"They've seen that on television, too," Parker said in a bitter voice.

*   *   *

Josiah Cardwell, the president of the Clayton Bank, looked like a man who didn't believe what he was hearing.

"You're talking in telephone numbers, Mr. Haviland," he said.

Cardwell was sitting by Haviland's desk in the town clerk's office. Haviland had taken off his glasses and was wiping them with his linen handkerchief. Fatigue and tension were beginning to catch up with him, but they didn't show in his manner or his voice.

"Let's talk about the mechanics of it first, Mr. Cardwell," Haviland said. "How long will it take you to get a half million dollars in tens and twenties together in one place? Here."

"We'd have to send out a call to banks all over the state," Cardwell said. "We'd be lucky to do it in a day."

"Half a day may be all we've got," Haviland said. "Possible?"

"It'll be a hell of a job."

"State troopers can carry the money from different banks. You make a dozen phone calls, we alert a dozen troopers. That's the mechanics of it."

"So maybe it can be managed," Cardwell said. "But we can't just hand out half a million dollars to people who can't pay it back. I'm a bank president, not a philanthropist."

"You know your town better than I do," Haviland said. "But I know there are a lot of well-heeled people in Clayton and Lakeview; quarry owners, factory owners, rich retired people. They're going to have to underwrite this ransom. I can't guarantee it, but the odds are we'll catch the kidnappers before they have a chance to spend much of it. But suppose we don't. The lives of a lot of people are on the line. Do you want the whole world to know this town didn't think those kids were worth saving?"

"But half a million dollars!"

"If one of the kids was yours?"

"You want to sell this idea of yours to a town meeting?"

"There isn't time for that," Haviland said. "Give me the names of ten people whose credit is good enough to raise fifty thousand dollars. I'll contact them. When I'm through I'll make public the list of those who were willing to go out on a limb to save those children." His lips tightened. "And I'll also make public a list of those who turned me down."

Cardwell stirred unhappily in his chair. "Well, I suppose there are ten or twelve people who might," he said. "I could begin with Tom Mowers, who owns the—"

"I thought of beginning with you, Mr. Cardwell," Haviland said. "I've seen that big house on the hill —when I was working the Johnsville case. And all that rich farmland, and that swimming pool."

Cardwell looked like a hooked fish. "I suppose I'd be willing," he said. "You really think you might get the ransom back if it's passed on to the kidnappers?"

"The FBI always gets its man," Haviland said. "You've seen that on television, haven't you, Mr. Cardwell? Nine other names, please."

Cardwell might be shamed into giving money, but what about the other wealthy men in the town? There wasn't much he could do until daylight except try his hand, Haviland thought. If he could sell one key person, it might make the rest fall into line.

In a few hours they would be inundated by reporters from all over the country, but at that moment there was only one newspaperman on hand —Lewis Hoag of the *County Press*, published in Lakeview. Hoag, a short, wiry little man with crewcut grey hair and a lined face that suggested he had laughed a lot in his time, was not only a reporter for the *Press*, he was also the owner and publisher. He had lived in the area all his life. He knew everybody in Clayton, Lakeview, and Johnsville.

"It's important to get to the right person, Mr. Hoag," Haviland said. "The right person, prepared to give generously, could give us a head start on the whole thing. I have a pledge from Josiah Cardwell and a list of names." He passed the piece of paper to the reporter.

"Josiah isn't your man," Hoag said, eyes twinkling. "He squeals each time a nickel slips through his fingers."

"I noticed that. I think he secretly hopes I don't make it, since that would relieve him of his pledge."

"Pledge for how much?" Hoag asked.

"Fifty thousand."

Hoag whistled. "Man, you must have twisted his arm good."

"That tactic won't work with nine others." Haviland pointed at the list. "Pick me out one man of compassion who doesn't equate loss of money with castration."

Hoag laughed. "The size of your weapon is made public by the size of your bank account," he said. Then he ran down the list with his ink-stained forefinger. "Not one of these men would be crippled by the loss of fifty Gs." His finger stopped near the bottom of the list. "Manfred Green," he said. "When he came here fifty years ago his name was Greenbaum. Fifty years ago Clayton, like a lot of places, was a hotbed of anti-Semitism, so Manny dropped the '-baum' from his name. It didn't help that much until later, when the climate changed. Manny made a fortune out of inventing some kind of areosol spray can. It's still pouring in.

"In the beginning, when he came here and bought a house, he heard himself called 'kike,' got anonymous letters in the mail telling him to leave town, had rocks thrown through his windows, was generally ostracized. Had a wife, I recall, a lovely young woman, and a baby son. Manny could take it for himself, but when his wife Rebecca got the treatment from the local ladies, he turned into an avenging angel. He had the weapon—money. He bought the local water company, got control of the local power plant, helped some of the quarry owners who were in trouble. Then he had the town by the short hairs. But just when he was ready to get even, a terrible thing happened to him. His wife and four-year-old son were killed in a railroad accident. That wiped out everything Manny cared about in the whole world. Rebecca and the boy died in the intensive care unit at the Lakeview hospital —they said it was because the hospital had inadequate equipment. People waited for Manny to lower the boom, sue for malpractice, whatever. Instead he contributed a huge sum of money to re-equip that intensive care unit.

" 'So it shouldn't happen to anyone else,' he said when people asked him why."

"Quite a man," Haviland said.

"I guess the community felt pretty guilty about Manny," Hoag said. "They expected him to punish them and instead he turned benefactor. He became a director of the bank. Later there was a new wing for the hospital—the Rebecca Green Annex. And through him our water is now fresher and cleaner, our power is more efficient. Manny Green has become a kind of local Santa Claus, operating year 'round. If Manny asks for money they're likely to give, because the older generation still feels guilty about him. I think he's your man."

"Let's go see him," Haviland said.

"At four o'clock in the morning?"

"Call him and tell him we're coming."

It was bitterly cold outside. Haviland thought about the missing children as Lewis Hoag drove him to Manfred Green's house. Where in God's name were they? Were they protected from this awful winter night?

Hoag pointed to a small, unostentatious house set back from the road. The windows were brightly lighted.

"Manny never went grand," Hoag said. "That's the house he and Rebecca bought when they first came here. He could afford a castle, but he's always stayed where he and his wife shared their lives."

Somehow Haviland had expected to see a small, wizened man. Manfred Green was big, with a mane of white hair and large bushy eyebrows. He opened the front door wearing a heavy flannel bathrobe over pajamas. His feet were encased in sheepskin-lined slippers. Behind him in the simple living room a fire burned brightly on a fieldstone hearth.

"Hello, Lew," he said. He had a deep, booming voice. His eyes were dark and warm.

"This is Clyde Haviland, in charge of the kidnapping case," Hoag said.

Green's handshake was firm. "Come in, gentlemen," he said. He led the way to chairs by the fireplace. "You've come to me for the ransom money?"

"What makes you think that?" Hoag asked.

"You don't pay a social call at this time of the morning to discuss the price of eggs," Green said. "Sit down, gentlemen."

Haviland explained the problem—how to find half a million dollars in a few hours. "I want to find ten people who will each underwrite fifty thousand dollars of that amount, Mr. Green. So far I have one."

"Who?" the old man asked.

"Josiah Cardwell."

The man's mouth twitched at a corner. "How did you manage that?"

"I shamed him into it," Haviland said.

"And you're planning to shame me into it too?"

"No, sir," Haviland said. "I hope to add you to the list and get you to shame some others."

Manny Green nodded slowly. "I don't know much about what's happened," he said. "Which children are involved?"

"Seven families, nine kids," Hoag said. "The Fred Williamses, the Ishams, the Gormans, the Trents, the Dave Nortons, and two kids each from the Dicklers and the Jenningses."

"Not much money there for certain," Green said. "What about the bus driver?"

"Jerry Mahoney? Right now half the town thinks he may be responsible."

"Mahoney isn't a Jewish name," Manny Green said.

"Jewish? Of course he's not Jewish."

"Our world is often ruled by prejudice, Lew," the

old man said. "If the driver were Jewish, or black, or Puerto Rican, I could understand the suspicion. But a good Irishman?"

Haviland and Hoag laughed.

"A somewhat bitter joke, gentlemen," Green said. His eyes closed. "I should help these people? You see, I know them all—and their fathers before them. Fred Williams's father was head of the zoning board when I first came to Clayton. He tried to get the sale of this house revoked—because I was a Jew. Isham's father and Roger Trent's father tried to block my purchase of the water company—because I was a Jew. Dave Norton's father was the president of the bank in those days. He tried to keep me from buying bank stock—because I was a Jew. Joe Gorman's father threw a rock through my front window—because I was a Jew. Karl Dickler's father sued me for trespassing on his land when I was out for a walk one summer day—because I was a Jew. The only one I don't know is Warren Jennings. He's had his own problems—because he's black."

We came to the wrong place, Haviland thought.

The old man opened his eyes. "Forty-five years ago I had a son and I lost him. That may seem a long time ago to you, but to me it's like yesterday. If my boy had been on that bus I'd have raised heaven and earth to ransom him. I'll get your money for you, Mr. Haviland—not to help the people who have mocked and hated me, but to help those children. Now, can I get you something warming to drink—coffee, brandy?"

"You've warmed me enough, Mr. Green," Haviland said, rising. "I have to get back on the job. I don't quite know how to express my gratitude."

"You have nothing to be grateful for, Mr. Haviland," Manny Green said. "I'm not doing this for you. You are a stranger. What I do is for the children, who are guilty of nothing."

Shortly after seven o'clock the first army helicopter appeared over Clayton. The hope was that from the sky they might be able to spot the missing bus hidden somewhere in the woods around the two towns. It seemed certain that the kidnappers would have abandoned it and shifted to other waiting vehicles. By eight o'clock three other copters were circling the area.

The parents of the missing children had gone home, as instructed by Haviland, but the rest of the citizenry of Clayton milled around the town, talking, wondering, guessing. Word got out that Haviland was trying to raise the ransom money, and there were instantly dozens of offers of help —a hundred dollars, fifty dollars, ten dollars. Sympathy for the parents was there, but these small donations wouldn't scratch the surface.

Haviland had been right about the rich men in the community. He found the nine men he needed to underwrite fifty thousand dollars each before ten o'clock that morning. A small army of troopers was on the road, bringing the money from a dozen banks in the state. By eleven o'clock the cash in tens and twenties was at the Clayton Bank.

When Haviland notified the seven families that the people of Clayton had come through for them, some of the parents wept in gratitude. It was a miracle of sorts. Several of the men whom Haviland had persuaded to help had gone further than he asked. When the right time came they would offer a substantial reward for information that would lead to the capture of the kidnappers.

Now came the torture of waiting. By eleven-thirty the people of Clayton and the authorities were ready to respond to instructions from the people who had their children. But no call came. Minutes dragged by like weighted hours. Parents huddled around telephones, praying for some word.

By one o'clock the tension was unbearable. Karl Dickler, unshaven, his eyes red from sleepless hours, had left his wife to cover their phone at home. He chose to wait in Haviland's office. He had to know that anything that could be done was being done. The schoolteacherish Haviland was beginning to get on Dickler's nerves. He just sat at his desk, waiting. There were half-hourly reports from the helicopter pilots. No sign of the bus. Surely if it were in the woods somewhere the copters, flying low over the tree tops, would find it.

"Road blocks or not," Sergeant Mason said, "they managed to slip through during the night. They could be in Ohio by now. Could they have had a way to repaint the bus somewhere so it wouldn't be noticed?"

"They're not in Ohio," Haviland said. "They're not that far away. They have to collect the money, don't they?"

"One of them could have been left behind for that," Mason said.

"You've come to think there are more than one?" Haviland asked. "You don't think it's just Jerry Mahoney?"

"I don't know what the hell I think," Mason said, bitterly.

Just before two o'clock in the afternoon, when despair was becoming unbearable, the call came. It came to Joe Gorman in his diner. The place was crowded with people, drinking coffee, talking, talking, when the wall phone in the corner of the diner rang.

"Listen, and listen carefully," a muffled voice said.

"Quiet!" Joe Gorman shouted. "This is it!"

The diner was suddenly deathly still.

"You have the money?" the muffled voice asked.

"Yes, we've got it."

"You will put it in a suitcase and you, Gorman, nobody else, will drive it out to the pay phone outside Hellstrom's Drive-In on Route 17. You will get another call there with instructions."

"What time am I supposed to be there?" Joe asked.

"We'll know when you're there, Gorman."

"I need to talk to one of the children when I get there," Gorman said. "I can't turn over the money without talking to one of the children."

The dial tone sounded in his ear. The caller hadn't heard that last plea, or had ignored it.

A dozen men ran down the street with Gorman to the town clerk's office. The word had come.

"We stake out Hellstrom's place," Mason said.

Haviland took a deep drag on his inevitable cigarette. "They'll know," he said. "If they'll know when Joe arrives, they'll know if we have the place covered." He reached for the phone on his desk. "What kind of a car do you drive, Joe?"

"Jeep," Joe Gorman said.

"Color?"

"Dark green."

"Top on it or open?"

"Top."

"Somebody get some white paint," Haviland said. "I want to mark a white cross on the top of that jeep." He began to dial a number.

"What the hell for?" Mason asked.

"We can't follow Gorman openly, or stake out Hellstrom's, but the helicopters can follow him," Haviland said. He was connected with the airfield and gave his instructions. When he put down the receiver he looked straight at Gorman.

"You'll go to Hellstrom's and wait for the call. You may have to wait awhile. Don't stand around looking up at the sky! When you get your instructions just take the money where they tell you and leave it. A copter will follow you and it will circle around till someone comes to pick up the cash."

"Couldn't I call you to tell you where I'm supposed to go?"

"If they know when you arrive, they'll know what you do. Stop to make a phone call and the ball game is over."

"Don't I insist on them telling me where we can find the kids?"

"You can ask," Haviland said, "but they aren't going to tell you. When they have the money and get clear of the area they may let us know where the kids are. If," and Haviland's face was grim, "they intend to play ball."

"And if they don't?"

"When that time comes we'll decide what to do. Your job is to deliver the cash, Joe. Good luck, and play it cool."

The white cross had been painted on the top of the jeep and the money placed in a large black suitcase. A dozen men were eager to follow Joe Gorman in their cars, but Mason and Teliski put a stop to that.

Hellstrom's Drive-In was about six miles out of Clayton on Route 17, another favorite stop for truckers passing through. Joe Gorman, carrying a half million dollars in tens and twenties, headed for it in his jeep with the white cross painted on its top. He was aware of two helicopters circling overhead. He was thinking of his son, Peter. Pete was a gutsy little kid, but it was hard to imagine how he and the rest of the children were bearing up in the situation. Maybe by tonight he would be home safe, please God.

Joe Gorman pulled the jeep into the parking lot outside Hellstrom's. He took the suitcase with the money in it and walked across the lot to the glassed-in pay phone just outside the door to the drive-in.

He waited.

He waited fifteen or twenty minutes and there was no call. He could hear the helicopter overhead and he fought against the urge to look up. He could feel sweat running down inside his clothes, despite the clear, cool day. Why the hell didn't they call? They'd said they'd know when he got here.

Half an hour passed, and still nothing.

Joe wanted to call Haviland, but he'd had strict instructions not to. He might be seen. How long did these sonsofbitches expect him to wait? He realized he was pressing his leg hard against the suitcase with a half million dollars in it. He wondered if someone might turn up and snatch it away from him. Half the town of Clayton knew what was in the suitcase. Some crazy bastard might try to take advantage of that.

Then he heard a police car siren coming down Route 17 toward the drive-in. It was Teliski. He got out of the police car with its blinking top-lights and came over to Gorman.

"We blew it," he said.

"How do you mean?" Joe Gorman said.

"They knew we painted a cross on the top of

your jeep. They knew the helicopters were watching. They called Haviland."

"Jesus!"

"We're to take the money back to town and wait to hear. They say they'll give us one more chance."

"How did they know?" Gorman asked.

"Haviland thinks there must be someone right in town watching us."

"There aren't any strangers around," Gorman said. "We've had an eye out for strangers."

"I know," Teliski said, his mouth tight. "Haviland thinks someone in Clayton, someone we know, who belongs there, is in cahoots with them. Only way they could have got the word so quick."

"Who, for God's sake?"

"Karl Dickler has no doubts about it," Teliski said. "He's back on Jerry Mahoney, with his father, Pat, and the Deering girl letting Jerry know what's cooking."

"Haviland buy that?"

"He's goddamned well got to consider it," Teliski said.

CHAPTER FIVE

Trooper Sam Teliski carried the suitcase containing the money back to Clayton. Joe Gorman wanted no responsibility for it. God, how smart they were—or how stupid we are, Joe thought. They had someone in town watching, letting them know in advance just what was planned.

Following the police car in his jeep, Joe Gorman found himself wondering about Pat Mahoney and Liz Deering. It was hard for him to believe that the old man and Liz, respected and liked by everyone in town, could be in on such a scheme. And how could they have known about the white cross on his jeep top, placed there to guide the helicopters? It had been a spur-of-the-moment idea of Haviland's. Trooper Teliski had found the paint that Joe Gorman had for touching up things in the diner. He'd painted the cross on the top while the jeep was still parked behind the diner. There hadn't been anyone watching him. Everyone was crowded around the town clerk's office, waiting for news. Teliski had brought the jeep there. No one could see the painted cross on the top unless they'd been looking out a second-story window. Pat Mahoney's house was a mile away.

Joe Gorman remembered walking out of the town clerk's office with the suitcase full of money. The crowd outside were all people he knew. All the parents of the missing children had been there, praying for his success—the Williamses, the Ishams, the Jenningses, Josephine Dickler, the Trents, the Nortons. Karl Dickler had been right beside Joe as he came out. He remembered thinking at the time that the only people involved who weren't there were Pat Mahoney and Liz Deering. You couldn't miss old Pat with his white, white hair and his flashy oddball clothes. Joe was sure he hadn't seen Liz Deering. He'd thought at the time they were the only people involved who were missing.

Joe wanted to stop at O'Brien's Bar for a drink, but he evaded the temptation. A drink would have helped to steady his nerves, which weren't what they ought to be, but he knew if he were called on to deliver the money again he'd best be cold sober.

An uncomfortable thought began to creep into Joe Gorman's head. Could there have been someone in Haviland's office who had heard exactly what the investigator planned? Someone who heard him order the white cross painted on the jeep? Someone who heard him alert the army helicopters to follow it? Joe tried to remember exactly who had been there. There'd been Haviland, and Sheriff Peabody, and the troopers Mason and Teliski, and Karl Dickler, and Jimmy Craven, Jerry Mahoney's boss. Could any one of them have been a traitor, a villain, a passer-on of critical information? You had to eliminate Haviland himself. You had to assume the troopers could be trusted. Or could you eliminate anyone with so much money involved? The squealer, whoever he was, had to be in for a share of it. Any man might have his price when you get up into six figures.

It might have interested Joe Gorman to know that Haviland was thinking along much the same lines. The more he toyed with the problem that faced him the more Haviland began to categorize the whole affair as an "inside job." Clayton was not a town, a place, an outside criminal would pick for a job. Except for a dozen or so people it wasn't a town of riches. There must be many better places to hit for big money than Clayton. One child from one very rich family somewhere would have been much easier to handle than this elaborate, complex maneuver. Every step of this bizarre business required knowledge of the town, knowledge of daily routines. The kidnappers had to know exactly what the bus schedule was. They had to know its route. They had to know when it would go into the dugway. However they had managed its disappearance, they had had to know exactly when and where to strike. They had to know the town well enough to feel sure the whole town would come up with the ransom. They had to know the countryside well enough to disappear in broad daylight with nine children, a driver, and a bright yellow bus clearly marked.

The reason for choosing Clayton and Clayton's children had to be because this was where the kidnappers lived, because they knew it inside out, every twist and turn, every resource. More and more Haviland was convinced of this, and while he waited, he wondered who was rubbing elbows with him, smiling at him, offering help, while kill-

ing every move the authorities made. Faces began
to drift before Haviland, faces of people he had
automatically trusted and with whom he had been
open and frank, counting on their help. The faces
belonged to the same people Joe Gorman was thinking about as he headed back to the town clerk's
office in his jeep—the sheriff, the troopers, Karl
Dickler, Jimmy Craven. There were two others to
whom Haviland wasn't yet able to put faces because he hadn't met them, Pat Mahoney and Liz
Deering. And there was one other Haviland
thought about that Joe Gorman hadn't—Joe Gorman.

Trooper Teliski brought in the suitcase, handling
it as though it might contain a bomb.

Joe Gorman really had no story to tell. He had
gone straight to the phone booth at Hellstrom's,
had waited by the phone booth, hadn't looked up
once at the sky, dotted with helicopters. He had
waited and waited until Teliski showed up with the
news.

"I swear I didn't give it away," he said.

"I'm sure you didn't," Haviland said, polishing
his glasses with that white linen handkerchief. "I
have to tell you all something. I was surprised
when we got instructions to deliver the money in
broad daylight. They must have known those helicopters had been in the air for hours, in constant
touch with us. They must have known it would be
easy for us to follow anyone who was delivering
the ransom. I had expected we would be told to
deliver after dark, when we couldn't follow our
man unnoticed—car headlights—and when they
could pick up the money where it was dropped
without being seen, or at least being aware if we
set some kind of trap for them. But we had to fol-

low instructions. I'm not surprised at the outcome."

"What are you going to do now?" Karl Dickler asked, his voice harsh, his hand clutching at his cheek.

"There's only one thing we can do," Haviland said, putting his glasses back on. "Wait."

"Well, I tell you what I'm going to do," Dickler said. "I'm going to see Pat Mahoney and make the little sonofabitch tell us what's going on."

"You're out of your skull," Jimmy Craven said angrily. "The Mahoneys have nothing to do with this."

"Well, name me someone then," Dickler shouted back. "Name me someone in this town!"

No one said anything. The room was suddenly still.

Haviland lit a cigarette and took a deep drag on it. "I guess it's time I talked to Mr. Mahoney and the girl," he said. "Not you, Dickler. Not in your state of mind. And I want you at home by your phone. There's another call coming and it may come to you. Teliski, you man the phone here. Sergeant Mason and I will go have a chat with Pat Mahoney."

Liz Deering, Jerry Mahoney's girl, was sick with anxiety. Jerry was foremost in her mind—Jerry missing with the children; Jerry, worse than that, suspected by his friends. But on top of that there was old Pat Mahoney. She was very fond of the old man, and he hadn't made the slightest sense since the night before when the angry people had left his house. When the news came that there had been a ransom demand and it might be met, he had reacted to it with hope, or satisfaction. He seemed lost somewhere in the past. Liz thought it was probably something that happened to old people in crisis. They can't face the present, and they fall back on their dreams.

Pat had talked on endlessly about the old days in vaudeville. He seemed obsessed by the memory of the first time he had seen The Great Thurston in Sioux City. He remembered card tricks and sawing the lady in half and his wife Nora's childish delight in being completely bewildered. He seemed to be recalling everything he had seen the great magician do. Right now he was up in the attic, going through old trunks, looking at old costumes and pictures of the glory days of Mahoney & Faye. He knew but seemed unconcerned about the fact that ransom money had been demanded, raised, and that someone was on the way to deliver it. It was as if he had blotted Jerry's danger out of his mind as the only way to bear it. No matter how hard she tried, Liz hadn't been able to bring Pat back to the present. The tragedy seemed to have tipped him right out of the world of reason.

When Liz heard firm steps on the front porch and a sharp knock on the door she felt a surge of relief. There would be news of the children and Jerry. When she opened the door and saw Sergeant Mason and a tall, bespectacled stranger, her relief turned to fear. The police could only be bringing bad news, she feared.

"They've found them?" she asked Mason.

The sergeant shook his head. He was less aggressive than he had been on his first visit. This heightened Liz's fear. She felt certain he was trying to soften some kind of blow.

"There's no news," Mason said. "We weren't able to deliver the money. Something went wrong. We have to wait for later instructions." He introduced and identified Clyde Haviland, who took off his hat and bowed politely. "We need to talk to you and Pat."

"Pat's in the attic," she said. "He's going through old souvenirs. I—I think I should tell you about him."

"Where were you when Joe Gorman took off with the ransom money?" Mason asked.

"Here with Pat," Liz said. "I didn't dare leave him. Jimmy Craven phoned us about what was happening. Pat—Pat didn't seem interested."

"You didn't dare leave him?" Haviland asked, in a gentle voice.

"He hasn't been himself since you were here last night," Liz said. "I think he just can't bear thinking about Jerry and the danger he must be in."

"We'd like to talk to him," Mason said.

"First, perhaps, we could talk to Miss Deering," Haviland said. "May we come in?"

Liz opened the door and led them into the living room. Haviland glanced around the room, interested by the dozens of photographs of old vaudeville stars. He had seen some of them perform when he was a kid.

"I think we should put this right on the line to you, Miss Deering," he said. "The further we get into this case, the more convinced we are that it has been engineered by someone in Clayton."

"That doesn't seem possible!"

"Nothing else seems possible," Haviland said. "There are quite a few people who, knowing that, believe Jerry has to be involved."

"That's crazy, Mr. Haviland!"

"You cover every angle in a case like this, no matter how unlikely," Haviland said. "I could be devious, Miss Deering. Or I could play it tough, sit you down in a chair, turn a bright light on your face, and shout questions at you. Like on television." He smiled at her.

"And you expect me to tell you that Jerry kidnapped the children and that Pat and I expect to share the ransom money with him?" Outrage changed Liz's voice to a stage whisper.

"I don't expect you to tell me that, whether it's true or not," Haviland said. "Whoever has the children has us over a barrel. We have to wait to hear from them again. We have to follow their instructions when they come. But afterward— after the children are free—there is no way in God's world the kidnappers can get to spend the money. The local authorities, the state police, the FBI will close in on them just as sure as God made little green apples."

Liz had got her breath back. She stood very straight, eyeing Haviland steadily. "You don't know us, Mr. Haviland. You don't know Jerry. If you did, you'd be ashamed of what you're suggesting."

A gutsy girl, Haviland thought.

"You say Craven called you to tell you the money was being delivered by Joe Gorman?" Mason cut in.

"Yes."

"Did he tell you a white cross had been painted on the top of his jeep so the helicopters could follow him?"

"A white cross?"

"So it would be easily spotted from the sky."

"Jimmy didn't tell me that. He just said the money was being delivered and the children and Jerry should be free soon." She looked back at Haviland. "That's not true, I take it."

"It was what we thought when Craven called

you," the investigator said. "But they found out what we were up to. We can only hope it will work out on the next try."

"So no one came for the money?" It was a voice from the kitchen doorway.

Haviland turned to look at Pat Mahoney. He had been prepared for Pat but not adequately. The flashy suit, the gaudy vest and tie, the huge diamond ring didn't belong in a small country town.

Mason introduced Haviland. "Mr. Haviland is a special investigator from the attorney general's office."

Pat's eyes brightened. "Say, you're the fellow that solved that murder over in Johnsville, aren't you? Smart piece of work."

"Thanks," Haviland said.

"Sit down, fellows," Pat said. "Maybe Liz would make us some coffee if we asked her pretty."

Liz, walking proud and straight, went out into the kitchen. Haviland sat down on the couch opposite Pat's big armchair. Mason stood by the windows, looking out at the street. Haviland offered Pat a cigarette.

"Don't smoke," Pat said. "Never really liked anything but cigars. Nora hated the smell of 'em, so what was I to do? You go to vaudeville in the old days, Mr. Haviland?"

"When I was a kid," Haviland said, lighting his cigarette. "I never had the pleasure of seeing you, though, Mr. Mahoney."

"Call me Pat," Pat said. "Everyone does. I was nothing, Mr. Haviland—just a third-rate song and dance man. But Nora—if you ever saw my Nora—"

Haviland waited for him to go on, but Pat seemed suddenly lost in his precious memories.

"You must be very worried about your son," Haviland said.

For a fractional moment the mask of pleasant incompetence seemed to be stripped from Pat's face. "Wouldn't you be?" he asked, harshly. Then, almost instantly, the mask was fitted back into place and old Pat gave his cackling laugh. "The payoff didn't work?"

"We bungled it," Haviland said. "We tried to follow Joe Gorman, who had the money, and they knew it."

"That's why you think someone local's involved?"

"You know we think that?"

Pat laughed like a delighted child. "Ever since I was a kid I've known that the best way to find out anything important is to eavesdrop."

"You heard what we said to Miss Deering?"

"It's my house," the old man said, his eyes narrowed. "I got a right to know what goes on in it."

Mason turned impatiently from the window. "It's my town and I got a right to know what goes on in it."

"I'm not in love with your town just now, Sergeant," Pat said. "They think Nora's boy would harm their children. How is it no one came to me when they were trying to raise money for the ransom? I'd have chipped in this diamond ring. It's got Jerry out of trouble more than once."

"He's been in trouble before?" Haviland asked, quietly.

"His main trouble was his Pop," Pat said. He looked back into the past again. "Sometimes there wasn't enough to eat, but we could always raise eating money on this ring." Then he turned his bright laughing eyes directly on Haviland. "You figured out how the bus disappeared?"

"No," Haviland said.

"Of course it doesn't really matter, does it?" Pat said. "It's what's going to happen now that matters."

"You mean paying the ransom and getting the children and Jerry back safe."

"If that's what's going to happen," Pat said. The cackling laugh suddenly grated on Haviland's nerves. Maybe the old joker did know something.

"You have a theory about what's going to happen?" Haviland asked, curbing his exasperation.

"You ever see The Great Thurston on the Keith–Orpheum circuit?" Pat asked.

"I'm afraid not," Haviland said.

"Greatest magic act I ever saw," Pat said. "Better than Houdini. Better than anyone. I first saw him in Sioux City—"

"About the case here," Haviland interrupted. "You have a theory?"

"I got no theory," Pat said. "But I know what's going to happen."

Haviland leaned forward. "What's going to happen?"

"One of two things," Pat said. "After the ransom is paid and you've lost your money, and you still haven't got the kids and Jerry back, everybody in this town is going to be looking in the lake for that station wagon, where they know it isn't, or in the dugway woods, where they know it isn't. That's one thing that may happen. The other is that everybody stays at home, waiting for a new demand, or some new news. There's one same result from both things, isn't there?"

"Same result?"

"Sure. Nobody in Clayton goes to work. The quarries don't operate. The small businesses will shut down. People will be looking or people will be waiting—"

"So?"

"So what good will that do anyone?"

Haviland ground out his cigarette in an ash tray. "It won't do anyone any good. The quarries will lose some money. The small businesses will lose some money."

"You're missing the point, Mr. Haviland," Pat said. "The disappearing bus is a magic trick. The magician is getting the people to do what he wants, act like he wants."

"The magician?"

"If we knew the answer to that it would all be over," Pat said.

Just then Liz Deering came back with three mugs of steaming coffee.

"There isn't much point to what you're saying, Pat," Haviland said.

Pat's eyes twinkled. "You said you never saw The Great Thurston."

"I never saw him."

"Well, we'll see. If they're supposed to stay home and wait, people will stay home and wait. If they're supposed to be out searching, they'll be out searching. Ah, coffee smells good, Liz. Pull up a chair, Sergeant. By the way, Mr. Haviland, I'll make you a bet."

"I'm not a betting man," Haviland said.

"Oh, just a manner-of-speaking bet," Pat said. "I'll make you a bet that tomorrow morning they'll be out searching. I'll make you a bet that even if you order them to stay home, they'll be out searching."

"Look here, Pat, if you know something—"

That dreamy look came back into Pat's eyes. "Nora was so taken with The Great Thurston that time in Sioux City that I went around to see him after the show. He was real complimentary about Nora. He'd heard her sing. A regular nightingale, he called her. I thought maybe he'd show me how to do a few simple tricks. I told him it was for Nora, but I really thought we might use 'em in our act. He wouldn't tell me anything; that is, not about his tricks. But he told me the whole principle of his business."

"Sugar?" Liz asked Haviland. Poor old man, she thought.

"The principle is," Pat said, "to make your audience think only what you want them to think, and see only what you want them to see." His eyes brightened. "Which reminds me, there's something I'd like to have you see, Mr. Haviland."

The old man was up out of his chair and standing at the foot of the stairs. Haviland gulped his coffee. Somehow he felt mesmerized by Pat Mahoney. He followed him.

Liz Deering looked at Sergeant Mason and there were tears in her eyes. "It's thrown him completely off base," she said. "You know what he's going to show Mr. Haviland?"

Mason shook his head.

"A cowboy suit," Liz said, and dropped down on the couch, crying softly. "He's going to show him a cowboy suit."

And she was right. Haviland found himself in the attic, his head bowed to keep from bumping into the sloping beams. Old Pat had opened a wardrobe trunk and, with the gesture of a waiter taking the silver lid off a tomato surprise, revealed two cowboy suits, one hanging on each side of the trunk. They were Nora's and his, he explained. Chaps, shirts, vests, boots, Stetsons, and gun belts —all studded with stage jewelry.

"—And when the lights went out," Pat was saying, "all you could see was these gee-gaws, sparkling. And we'd take out the guns—" And suddenly Pat had two six-shooters in his hands, twirling them and spinning them. "In the old days I could draw these guns and twirl 'em into position faster than Jesse James!"

The spell was broken for Haviland. The old guy was cuckoo. "I enjoyed seeing them, Mr. Mahoney, but now I have to be getting back—"

CHAPTER

SIX

Haviland and Sergeant Mason drove back across town to the headquarters in a police car. It was going on five o'clock and the village was already bathed in gray of twilight, snow on the hills above them touched by the scarlet of a sunset. It was almost twenty-seven hours since the bus had disappeared in the dugway. Haviland realized he hadn't had any sleep since the night before last. He felt old.

"He flimflammed you out of putting any kind of heat on him," Sergeant Mason said. "Crazy like a fox, I think."

Haviland took off his glasses and pressed his fingers against tired eyelids. "Sometimes I think I'm a good cop and sometimes I think I'm a lousy one," he said. "I play hunches, and that's not good police work. But for me it's paid off. I've been lucky, because my hunches are very seldom wrong. I haven't written off Jerry Mahoney; maybe he's the magician the old man was talking about behind all this. But every instinct I have tells me that Pat Mahoney and Liz Deering are as innocent as my twelve-year-old daughter."

"I didn't know you had a kid."

"Maybe that will explain to you how badly I want to get the sonsofbitches responsible for this." Haviland replaced his glasses and leaned his head back against the seat. "You think the old man was just prattling about his dreams? Jesus, when he started twirling those guns for me up in the attic—"

"The girl says he's really gone to pieces."

"I don't think so," Haviland said, slowly. "I think the only thing in the world that matters to him is getting his son back and clearing his name."

"All that crap about The Great Thurston!"

"He said something that's true, you know. The disappearance of that bus was a magic trick. We just haven't made sense in trying to figure it out."

"Like he said, what does it matter how it was done as long as the kids are returned?"

" 'If that's what's going to happen,' " Haviland said, quoting the old man.

Mason turned his head and the car skidded slightly. "You think it isn't going to happen?"

"Are there any wild kids in this town?" Haviland asked. "Kids that are out for kicks?"

"No more, no less than any other town," Mason said. "For a while the high school kids went in for drugs. Today it's more booze than that. Why do you ask?"

"Hunch," Haviland said. He shivered as though he were cold, although the car heater kept things snug. "I have a feeling that when we make the payoff we're not going to see those children. I hope to God I'm wrong. But they've been holding those kids and Jerry Mahoney for more than twenty-four hours. No way they won't be able to describe the kidnappers well enough for us to nail them. They can't let the kids and Jerry go if they hope to spend their money."

"Oh, God," Mason said.

"We've all sold ourselves on the idea that it's someone local. Descriptions would have them caught in an hour. How can they turn the kids back?"

"If you're right, they could be dead now," Mason said in a flat voice.

"I know." Haviland straightened up. "Let's keep this to ourselves, Mason. There's no use driving a knife into the parents before it's necessary."

And now it was dark.

A couple of hundred townspeople milled around outside the town clerk's office, waiting for news. There had been some early hopes that Haviland, who had performed a miracle in Johnsville, might duplicate his success in Clayton. Those hopes were fading. The children were out there in the hands of completely callous villains, out there in freezing weather. More than one person in the crowd had begun to share Haviland's unspoken fear that the children would never be seen again alive, money or no money. No one mentioned this fear; it could start a kind of hysteria, be unendurable for the parents.

In the office Haviland sat behind his desk, a drooping statue, waiting for the phone to ring. Someone would have to hear soon. Darkness was the kidnappers' ally.

In addition to the crowd of locals outside the office there was a small army of out-of-town news-paper, radio, and television reporters. These, armed with cameras, tape recorders, and shortwave radio transmitters, had been assigned to the selectmen's office down the hall. Haviland had insisted his own headquarters be kept clear of everyone except the troopers, Sheriff Peabody, and Frank Parker, the FBI man. He had given a brief statement to the press. The first attempt to deliver the ransom had failed. He described their attempt to have Joe Gorman watched by helicopters. The ruse had been spotted. There would be nothing else to report until they heard from the kidnappers again, and not then till after the payoff had been made and the children released.

"Will you try to cover the delivery again?" Haviland was asked.

"No," Haviland said. "And you can help by making it quite clear in your radio and TV spots that this time we'll follow instructions to the letter, set no traps."

It was past the time for being clever, too long past, Haviland told himself. They would follow instructions, all right—they had no choice. But waiting for those instructions was an exhausting business. You turned the problem this way and that, worrying at it like a dog fencing at a woodchuck in a life-and-death struggle. You kept trying to find a place to take hold, a place where you could get a grip on it.

It *had* to be someone local, someone who knew the area, someone who knew the people of the town and how they would react. It had to be someone who had been certain that the town could raise the money. If they hadn't known, they'd never have demanded a ransom beyond the reach of the children's parents.

Haviland went down the hall to the room where

the press people waited and was instantly surrounded, buried under questions. He asked Lewis Hoag, the local man, to come back to his office.

"No special inside stuff—just for Hoag!" the press people shouted after him.

"Nothing special, I promise," Haviland said. "Mr. Hoag can supply me with information I need."

"Glad to get out of there," Hoag said, wiping his face with a red bandana. "They never let up with questions. Wish I had the answers."

One of the women clerks in the next office had filled and plugged in a coffee percolator for Haviland. He poured two mugs full and gave one of them to Hoag.

"Have to take it black," he said. "Happens to be no choice."

"That's fine," Hoag said.

"So I have some questions," Haviland said.

"Do my best." Hoag looked grateful for the coffee.

"Tell me about Joe Gorman," Haviland said.

"Joe? Not much to tell." Then Hoag chuckled. "I guess you can't really say that about anyone, can you? What is it you want to find out about him?"

"I don't know," Haviland said, unsmiling.

The little newspaperman leaned back in his chair and lit a crooked black stogie. "The Gormans came to town to work the quarry when that started to be big business in Clayton about fifty years ago. There was so much work the quarry owners had to import outside labor, and they brought in a lot of Irish from around Boston. Mike Gorman, Joe's father, was one of them."

"Is he the one who threw a rock through Manny Green's window?"

"The one," Hoag said. "He was a type; hard

working, hard drinking, a brawler and a woman chaser when he was drunk. On a Saturday night the local jail would be full of drunken quarry workers who'd been raising hell in Clayton and Lakeview. Mike Gorman spent a lot of weekends in the cooler. Then he married a local girl, had seven kids over the years. Joe was the youngest and the only boy, the apple of old Mike's eye. The girls were like all the girls in town, brought up to be wives. Eventually they all married, all but one of them to local boys. That one ran off with a traveling salesman; so far as I know, she never came back to Clayton. But young Joe was shaped by his father—a bright, hell-raising, mischievous kid. When he was old enough, he went to work in the quarries himself; on weekends he got drunk. Everybody liked Joe Gorman, but the respectable folk tried to keep their daughters locked up when he was around. There was a new scandal about young Gorman and some girl every week. Eventually he was seen a lot with Ethel McCormick, daughter of one of Mike's friends. She had no shame, people said, she flaunted her affair with Joe. Eventually, she couldn't help flaunting it. She was pregnant— this big—with his baby. I have to tell you I expected Joe to skip town. He wasn't the marrying kind. But he fooled us all."

"He married her?"

"Married her and changed his whole life." Hoag relit his chewed-on cigar. "He left the quarries, found the money somewhere to buy the local diner. Overnight he became a respected, hard-working family man. The baby is young Peter, now on that bus."

"Is Gorman still a drinker?"

"No more. Oh, Joe will take a drink or two at a party, but forget about those wild benders he used to go on."

"An ideal citizen," Haviland said drily.

"You better believe it. He keeps the diner open seven days a week, only takes off a day or two during hunting and fishing seasons, leaving the diner to his short order cook and his wife. Joe loves to hunt and fish."

Haviland was silent for a moment. "Which means he must know the whole countryside intimately."

"I'd say so."

"He wouldn't need a map if they picked an out-of-the-way place they wanted the money delivered to."

Hoag's eyes widened. "You're right."

"They knew the right man to choose to deliver the money, then," Haviland said.

"So there was a reason for choosing him," Hoag said.

A little after seven o'clock Karl Dickler walked into Haviland's office. He leaned on the back of a chair as if he'd been running.

"I've heard from them," he said in a choked voice.

The men in the office crowded around him.

"Call came at five minutes to seven," Dickler said. "I'm to deliver the money."

"Where?" Sergeant Mason asked.

"I'm not to tell you, not to tell anyone," Dickler said.

"For Christ's sake, Karl!"

"They said if I told anyone they'd send me a piece—a piece of Dorothy, like an ear, or a finger with her ring on it."

"Jesus!" Mason said.

"Does your daughter wear a ring?" Haviland asked.

Dickler nodded. "A school ring. All the girls wear school rings. It's some kind of a club." His voice was a hoarse whisper. "You've got to let me take the money and deliver it. You've got to keep anyone from trying to follow me."

"We'll guarantee not to follow you, but we have to know where you're going," Haviland said.

Dickler shook his head, stubbornly. "I'm going to do exactly what they told me. I've got two kids out there. I didn't even tell my wife; I was afraid you might pressure her into telling. Please, Haviland, it's the only chance we've got. They told me that. Last chance, they said."

Haviland looked around at the troopers, the sheriff, the FBI man. "Do we have any choice?" he asked.

"Did you ask them for some proof the children are alive?" the FBI man asked.

"No," Dickler said. "I have to believe they are."

"Do you expect to contact them?"

"I'm just to deliver the money to a certain place and go away. I've got to start now. I'm supposed to deliver at eight o'clock. I've only just enough time."

Forty minutes till eight o'clock. Twenty-five, thirty miles, Haviland thought. A cold night wind rattled the window panes in the office.

"Give him the suitcase," Haviland said. "Where's your car?"

"Out back. I didn't want people to see me driving up."

"Good. The troopers will see that no one follows you."

Teliski produced the suitcase filled with money and gave it to Dickler.

"One more thing, Mr. Dickler," Haviland said. "As soon as you've delivered the money, get to the nearest telephone you can find and let us know. Perhaps then you'll tell us where it is. Someone will be ready to pick it up as soon as you leave it. We need to be able to move as soon as we can."

"When they turn the children loose," Dickler said.

"Don't wait for that!"

"I've got to, Mr. Haviland. Don't you see, I've got to!" The nerve in Dickler's cheek was twitching wildly.

Haviland stood, rigidly silent for a moment. "Play it your way," he said, finally. "And good luck."

Mason and Teliski went out the front way, Dickler the back. Haviland sank slowly back into his chair behind the desk. He'd had no choice, had he? If his Nancy had been one of the missing children he'd have insisted on following instructions. You didn't bargain or make demands. They'd tried to be clever with the jeep and the helicopters and where had it got them?

Half an hour later Mason and Teliski came back to the office.

"No one out front got wise," Mason said. "None of the press people either."

"I think he headed out Route 17," Teliski said. "It's crazy not to follow him."

"You haven't got any kids out there," Haviland said. He looked at Parker. "You agree we had to play it this way, don't you?"

Parker nodded. "There are times in cases like

this when you just have to wait. The kidnap victim comes first. Once we get the kids back—"

"Or know what's happened to them," Haviland said grimly.

"You think—?"

"If we're right about its being a local job, I'm afraid it's too late for the kids." It was the first time he'd expressed his fears to anyone but Mason. The others looked shocked.

"So they walk away with the money and leave us ten dead people!" Teliski said.

"Or nine," Sheriff Peabody said. "I still haven't written off Jerry Mahoney. He could be one of the ones who walks away."

"Not far," Haviland said.

Nine o'clock.

It was going to take Dickler forty minutes to get wherever he was going, Haviland thought. Maybe a few minutes on foot. Then another forty minutes to come back. They should be hearing from him soon.

Ten o'clock.

Men looked at watches. There was little or no conversation. Haviland was out of his chair, pacing the office, fighting an overwhelming need for sleep.

"Something's gone wrong," Parker said.

"He may have been instructed to wait somewhere for the kids," Haviland said.

"You think he came face to face with them?"

"They may have left a note for him at the spot he was to drop the money. Maybe he was told not to contact us until he had the kids."

"You don't really believe that, do you?" Parker said.

Haviland's bloodshot eyes were unblinking behind his spectacles. "No," he said.

"Well, for Christ's sake then!" Teliski exploded.

"We'll give him another hour," Haviland said, "and then I think we'd better start searching the countryside within a radius of thirty miles."

Mason didn't wait an hour to alert a dozen trooper cars. He'd be ready when Haviland gave the word.

At eleven-thirty Haviland made his decision. "Let's get it started," he said.

There were only five roads out of Clayton— Route 17, Route 4, Route 112, a dirt road that led up over the hills toward Johnsville, and the dugway to Lakeview. Dickler drove a dark green Chevrolet Nova, and its description was circulated to the troopers.

The unusual number of trooper cars suddenly had the crowd outside the building and the press people alerted. Something was up. The press people crowded into Haviland's office. Had he heard from the kidnappers? Why so many troopers out on the road?

Haviland's nerves were stretched thin, but he managed to hang onto his quiet, undisturbed manner.

"We're doing what we can to get the children back," he said. "I can't tell you what's cooking because we can't risk having you and dozens of townspeople getting in our hair. It's a touchy business, and it has to be handled by experienced people."

"But you've heard from the kidnappers?"

"Yes, I can tell you that much. We have new instructions from them. That's all I can tell you."

Haviland elbowed his way through the crowd to

his car, saying no more than he'd said to the press. He drove off, circled the town, and came back to a house not far from where he'd started. It was Karl Dickler's house. The windows were brightly lit. Haviland had literally only reached for the door knocker when the door opened and he was faced by Josephine Dickler.

"Mrs. Dickler, I'm Clyde Haviland, in charge of—"

"I know who you are," the woman said. "Is there any news?"

"Not yet. May I come in for a moment?"

"Of course."

A wood fire burned on a hearth opposite the front door. The room was simply furnished, but with a taste that must have been this woman's, Haviland thought.

"You haven't heard from Karl?" she asked.

"Not yet." And when Haviland saw terror spread over her face, he went on quickly, "There are any number of explanations for that, Mrs. Dickler. May I sit down? It's been a pretty exhausting day."

"Please," she said, gesturing toward an armchair by the fire.

"We expected to hear from your husband before this," he said, noticing that the clock on the mantle showed a few minutes to midnight. "We think that when he delivered the money he found some instructions for finding and freeing the children. He might not risk calling us till he had them safe."

"He said he wasn't going too far from Clayton," she said.

"The children could be miles away from the place he was told to drop the money."

"I can't bear any more of this," she said, her voice unsteady, her control almost gone.

"Karl told us that he hadn't told you where he'd been told to go," Haviland said.

"He didn't. They told him not to. After—after the mistake this morning, he was determined to do exactly what they told him to do."

"No hint?"

"Only that it wasn't too far from town."

"Like ten miles, twenty miles, thirty miles?"

"He just said not too far."

"It would be helpful if you had any sort of clue, Mrs. Dickler."

Her eyes widened. "You're worried about him. You think something—?"

"—may have gone wrong in finding the children. We'd like to find him, help him."

"I wish to God I could tell you something," she said.

"Your husband knows this countryside pretty well?"

"He was born and raised here," Josephine Dickler said.

"He hunt? Fish?"

"Every year in season. Why do you ask?"

"We still believe that somebody local is back of all this, Mrs. Dickler. They have chosen the person to deliver the money both times. Joe Gorman hunts and fishes. Your husband, too, you say."

"I don't understand what hunting and fishing have to do with it."

"A guess," Haviland said. "The kidnappers aren't going to pick up the money in some public place. They aren't holding the children in some easily spotted place. They never got to pass on instructions to Joe Gorman because they discovered our system for locating them. So this second time, because they no longer trust Gorman, they pick another man who knows the backwoods and inaccessible areas of the community just as well as Gorman did. It has to be someone local who knows those places. A cabin in the woods, a cave."

"Jerry Mahoney hunts with Karl every year," Josephine Dickler said. "He knows where places like that are, Mr. Haviland. He'd know where to take our children. May God strike him dead if he's the one!"

"Well, we can take hope from the fact that your husband will know where to look when he gets his instructions."

"He should be back by now. Shouldn't he, Mr. Haviland?"

Clyde Haviland stood up. The woman was on the edge of a crack-up, her two children and her husband missing.

"Your husband was determined to play this exactly as he was told, Mrs. Dickler. I guess I'd do the same thing if I were in his shoes," Haviland said. "He doesn't want there to be any slipup in getting the children back."

"How long will you wait before you start looking for Karl?"

Haviland hesitated. "We've already started looking for him," he said. "About a dozen trooper cars set out fifteen or twenty minutes ago."

"Then you don't believe he's just waiting for instructions somewhere!" she said, her voice rising.

"I want to make sure, Mrs. Dickler," Haviland said.

"Oh, my God!" she said, and sank down into a chair, weeping.

CHAPTER SEVEN

One o'clock.

Back in his office, Haviland waited. Sheriff Peabody had brought in a police radio, and he and Haviland could listen to the troopers talking back and forth to each other from their cars and to the dispatcher at the trooper barracks.

The search had produced nothing in the first hour and a half. Haviland was exhausted from waiting, doing nothing constructive himself. He got in touch with the phone company about one-thirty and asked for a list of pay phones within forty miles of Clayton. It turned out to be a monumental job. There were hundreds of them, counting wall phones in bars and restaurants and drugstores and other public places. Many of them would be inaccessible at this time of night—or morning to be exact. Haviland visualized one of those glassed-in booths outside a gas station or a place like Hellstrom's Drive-In. The kidnappers had picked such a phone for Joe Gorman; criminals had a way of duplicating patterns. The telephone supervisor promised a list of such phones as quickly as possible.

At 2:25 A.M. the log jam broke. A trooper out on Route 4 found Dickler's Chevrolet Nova pulled up in the shrubbery off a little side road that led to two small cottages.

"Looks like he parked there on purpose," the trooper reported. "He got out of the car and walked into the woods. But the wind's whipped up quite a bit out this way, Mr. Haviland, and whatever tracks Dickler left have had snow blown over them. Any trail he may have left has been obliterated."

"You say there are two cottages in there. Have you talked to the people?"

"One of them is closed up for the winter—people gone south. The other is occupied by an old couple named Wendall. They didn't see or hear anything."

"No one asked to use the phone, or for directions?"

"Nothing. No one came their way."

"Where, exactly, is Dickler's car?"

"About fifteen miles out of town on Route 4," the trooper said. "You pass Cooperman's Iron Works and about six-tenths of a mile past that there's this little side road on the right."

"Get some help there," Haviland said. "I'm on my way. Circulate in the woods. You may find there's someplace Dickler's trail wasn't blown over."

"Will do."

Haviland dialed Joe Gorman's number. Gorman answered on the first ring. Nobody in Clayton was doing much sleeping that night. Haviland told Joe where they'd found Dickler's car.

"Is there anything up in those woods, Joe?" he asked. "You know the country. A hunter's cabin, a cave, anything like that?"

"Let me think," Gorman said. "All I can remember is an old sap house up there, maybe a mile in."

"Sap house?"

"Lot of maple trees up there," Gorman said. "In the spring they tap them, take the sap up to this sap house to boil up into syrup. All there is is a sort of lean-to with some copper boilers and a woodshed."

"Could you take us to it?"

"Sure. You think that's where Karl was headed?"

"Unless you can think of a better place in that neighborhood. Get down here as quickly as you can. The kidnappers would probably want some kind of shelter while they waited for him—or a safe place to leave the suitcase, where it wouldn't be drifted over. Get moving, will you, Joe!"

At a few minutes past three Haviland and Joe Gorman reached Dickler's abandoned car. A trooper named Thornton was waiting there for them. He reported that three other men were trying to pick up Dickler's trail in the woods beyond, but so far no luck. He pointed to a walkie-talkie he was carrying.

"Gorman knows of a sap house up there that might fit the bill."

Gorman led the way, with Haviland and Thornton following. Thornton was contacting the other troopers on his walkie-talkie. About a mile in, Gorman had said. Climbing, it seemed much farther than that. Haviland wasn't wearing the right kind of shoes for a trek in the woods. Snow got inside them and his feet were freezing.

"Just up ahead," Gorman said finally.

By then Teliski and two other troopers had joined them in the climb. Wind whistled through the treetops and blew the light snow across their path in little gusts. There wasn't enough of it to drift, but it had successfully powdered over Dickler's trail if he had left one.

The sap house loomed up ahead in the moonlight, a weathered shack with a tar-paper roof. Haviland's heart jammed against his ribs. Lying on the ground, just outside the sap house, was something he was certain was a body, lightly powdered by blown snow.

Gorman and Trooper Thornton ran the last few yards and knelt beside the body. When Haviland reached it, Joe Gorman looked up at him, his face working.

"It's Karl," he said in a harsh voice.

Karl Dickler was very dead. His head had been beaten to a pulp, like a smashed Halloween pumpkin. In the cold it was impossible to tell how long ago it had happened.

Dickler's hands were broken and bloodied.

"He must have put up a hell of a fight," someone said.

There was a bloodstained piece of firewood a few feet from the body. It had been at least one of the weapons used to kill the man.

Teliski and the other troopers, spreading out, came to the conclusion, from various signs, that there had been at least two and maybe three men involved in the attack.

Haviland stood staring down at the body, his teeth clamped together to keep them from chattering in the cold. He was trying to reconstruct what might have happened. Dickler had obviously been instructed to bring the suitcase to the sap house. Three men were waiting there for him, or waiting nearby. If they had been waiting openly they must have been disguised—probably wearing ski masks, a popular television gimmick. Had Dickler handed them the suitcase and then asked about the children? As he talked had he recognized something familiar—a jacket, a scarf, a fancy pair of boots? Had he blurted out a name? If he had, they had had no choice but to kill him.

It could have been another way. He could have been instructed to leave the suitcase and go away. He had to know about the children. He had left, but being a skillful woodsman, he had circled back and waited. When someone, obviously two or three men, had come for the suitcase Dickler had burst out of his hiding place, demanding the return of his children. Perhaps the men were not disguised, thinking him gone. He would know them. He had to die.

There was an old sled in the sap house, evidently used for gathering firewood as well as for travel when the season for sapping was on, and Dickler's body, already stiff from the cold, was loaded on the sled and pulled by two troopers down the long slope to the side road. An ambulance was already there, alerted by the trooper's walkie-talkie radio. A dozen townspeople, and seven or eight of the trooper cars, were grouped around it.

You could sense a surging anger in the small crowd. There was only one reason in the world for Dickler to have been killed and everyone seemed to know it. He had recognized one or all of the kidnappers.

No one doubted Haviland's theory anymore. The whole ghastly business was a local job. Someone from Clayton had abducted the children and murdered Karl Dickler. A neighbor? Someone you had trusted and respected all your life?

Four A.M.

The ambulance carried Dickler's body to the Lakeview Hospital for examination by the coroner. Haviland, riding with Trooper Teliski, headed back to Clayton. The siren, wide open on Teliski's car, had a jangling effect on Haviland's already frayed nerves. He was thinking about Josephine Dickler. Who would break the news to her? Who would stay by her in this time of tragedy? She'd want to go to her husband, he suspected. She shouldn't be allowed to see him. There was very little of Karl Dickler's face left.

Back at the sap house Parker, the FBI man, had joined with the troopers in a widening search for the murderers' trail, or any kind of clue that might tell them something. The problem was darkness, the moon having faded out. Haviland had felt they should wait for daylight, but who could wait? He knew that by morning it would be a great stroke of luck if the searchers hadn't obliterated, like a herd of elephants, any trail they were looking for.

Rage, like a sickness, had infected even the trained personnel. They had goofed the day before while Gorman was trying to deliver the ransom. That had left them sitting around with their hands tied while Dickler traveled to his death. They were eager to find someone to punish, if they could lay their hands on him. And the more they were convinced that someone local was responsible, the more people mentioned Jerry Mahoney.

"I remember," Teliski shouted at Haviland over the wail of the siren, "—a year ago, it was. Some of the fellows who go hunting every fall had a cookout at that sap house. Venison steaks, they had. You know who did the cooking?"

"Don't tell me, I'll guess," Haviland said wearily. "Jerry Mahoney."

"Right on target," Teliski said. "They often cooked out there when they were after deer, because there was always good, dry firewood. Jerry knew that place, and every acre of ground around it. Like his own home!"

"So if he is our man, the kids are dead," Haviland said. "They'd have to know he was involved. No way he could let them talk later. I prefer to think—to hope—you're wrong, Teliski. I prefer to think we still have a chance of finding those children."

"It would be nice to believe in Santa Claus," Teliski said.

As they approached the town, Haviland thought for a moment that the town clerk's office was on fire. Flames lit up the whole square in front of the old stone building. Then, as the wailing trooper car began to pull in, he saw that people had built a huge bonfire in the center of the green, were crowded around to keep warm in the bitter cold. Five A.M. is usually the coldest hour of the darkness, and Peabody had said it would probably get down to about zero. It felt colder than that to Haviland, because his heart and his mind felt cold.

When the car stopped in front of the town clerk's office Haviland drew a deep, quavering breath. Television cameras were set up on either side of the entrance, and there were at least fifty reporters lying in wait for him. There was no way to duck them this time. The townspeople left their fire and crowded around him as he started to get out of the car.

Haviland held up his hands for silence. "You all know the news about Karl Dickler," he said.

There was an angry rumble from the crowd. Several of the reporters began shouting questions. Once more Haviland raised his hands for silence.

"I want to tell you one thing," he said. "The ransom was evidently delivered. At this moment there isn't one shred of evidence to suggest that the children have been harmed. I hope that we'll get some word from the kidnappers as to where to find them. If we don't, I hope the children will find their own way home, with Jerry Mahoney's help."

"Mahoney's gone with the money!" someone shouted.

"Our kids can't hope for any help from Mahoney!"

On the outer fringe of the crowd Haviland saw Liz Deering, the knuckles of one hand raised to her mouth as though she were chewing on them. Her pain was obvious.

"I haven't given up hope," Haviland said. "Don't any of you. Now there are things to do."

He wedged past the reporters and into his office, but there was no way to shake the ladies and gentlemen of the press. They crowded in after him, all asking questions at once. Behind his desk Haviland once more gestured for silence.

"I'll speak with you in a few minutes," he said. "No holds barred. But you've got to give me time to set some things in motion. You can stay here, quietly, or I'll have this office cleared."

They took him at his word; the clamor of voices simmered down to almost nothing. But they remained packed around his desk. Haviland turned to a white-faced Sheriff Peabody. Karl Dickler had been a close friend of the sheriff's.

"How many people live in Clayton?" he asked.

"Approximately twenty-five hundred," the sheriff said.

"That'd be what—seven hundred families?"

"Give or take a few."

"How many deputies and troopers can we get to check every damned family in town?"

"Couple of dozen," Peabody said. "Check 'em for what?"

"Who's missing, who's away, where they are. Who's unaccounted for tonight—last night and now."

"Take a couple of days!" Peabody said.

"We need answers by noon!" Haviland said.

"Not possible," Peabody said.

"There are nine kids and Jerry Mahoney out there somewhere. Make it possible." Haviland turned and gave the reporters a tired smile. "Your turn," he said.

The questions came in an avalanche.

Once again Haviland gestured for quiet. "Let me tell you first what we know," he said. "The kidnappers selected Joe Gorman and then Karl Dickler to deliver the ransom because they were hunters and knew the untraveled parts of the countryside. Right away that suggests someone who lives in this area —a local person who knew where the sap house was, and also knew who else would know where it was. We think Dickler was killed because he recognized the men who came for the ransom. Whether that person came openly and always meant to kill or whether Dickler penetrated a disguise and gave himself away—" Haviland shrugged. "We may never have the answer to that. Frank Parker of the FBI and I are both convinced that there were at least two men, possibly three, who worked over Dickler. I've asked the sheriff for a check of every family because I don't believe the kidnappers, if they're local people, have left town. To disappear now would be like a signed confession. I think they'll sit on the money until things cool down and the children have been returned."

"You don't think the FBI will come up with clues to the killers?" a man named Mercer from International News asked. Haviland knew him to be a top-flight investigative reporter.

"Too early to know," Haviland said. "It will be daylight in an hour or so. Not much hope of picking up a trail of any sort until then."

"You said the children may still be safe," Mercer said. "Do you believe that?"

"I believe what I want to believe, Mr. Mercer. And I'll keep on believing the children are safe and will be freed until I have some proof they aren't. There's nothing to indicate revenge against the town, or the parents. It seems to be a straightforward kidnapping case."

"But if the children can identify the kidnappers, won't you find them dead?" Mercer asked.

"We won't find them at all until the kidnappers have landed safely in Mexico or some other safe place."

"That could take a long time."

"You'd be surprised how long a man can go without food and water if he has to," Haviland said. "You know as much as I do now, ladies and gentlemen. We hope to pick up a trail at the sap house after daylight. We hope to get some word telling us where the children are. If not, we hope the children will free themselves before too long. We're going to check out every person in this town in the hope of turning up a clue. You have to wait and I have to wait. I haven't got the time or energy to speculate for you. You have all the facts we have. When there are more facts you'll get them."

"One last question," Mercer said.

"Shoot."

"Is the ransom money marked in some way?"

"Our instructions were not to mark it," Haviland said, his mouth tightening.

"But did you?"

"With the children's lives at stake would you expect us to disobey?"

"You're answering a question with a question," Mercer said. "Is the money marked? Do you expect to catch the kidnappers that way?"

"Mr. Mercer, the one thing we don't need are speculations from the press that will make the kidnappers nervous," Haviland said.

Trooper Teliski came into the office, elbowing his way through the army of reporters. "All hell's broken loose down the line," he said. "People are throwing rocks through Pat Mahoney's front windows."

"Oh, Jesus!" Haviland said.

Most of Haviland's adult life had been involved with crime. In recent years, as a special investigator for the Attorney General's office, he'd been in charge of murders and kidnappings, cases requiring his special expertise. The killings he knew best were crimes of passion, family violences that involved jealousy, greed, or revenge. Street killings, muggings, burglaries—they were for the regular police.

Haviland wondered now if he was the right person for the Clayton case. What experience did he have with twisted minds who'd use small children? His expertise had never covered *mindless* violence.

He'd always preferred his crime in neatly tied packages. And now he was faced with a mob. Damn it, handling that just wasn't his thing! *Damn it,* he said again, *you're a cop. You can do it. You did it once.*

He had been in Boston, following a lead on a homicide—a jealous wife had shot her husband. He remembered the case as if it were yesterday. He'd been walking along the street, minding his own business, deep in thought, when he'd heard the angry voices. He'd realized suddenly that he was standing across the street from a public school. A bus had pulled up and a group of black children were spilling out of it onto the sidewalk. Some white children and their mothers were screaming curses at the blacks, and some of them were being pushed and shoved around. From Haviland's side of the street a few black adults had appeared, no doubt parents and friends of the black children. They moved menacingly across the street. Haviland saw that some of them were armed with clubs, and he saw the glitter of the sun against the blade of a knife.

School busing and its attendant problems had never been a concern of Haviland's. He had no convictions about it one way or another. All he saw now was the violence. Instinctively he moved across the street. Children, both black and white, were caught between two angry groups of adults. A small black boy was picked up by a white man and tossed aside like a sack of garbage. Two little black girls were clinging together, crying. Haviland reached out, put his arms around them, looking around for some sign of police, some symbol of order. A black man, his face distorted with anger, bore down on Haviland.

"Keep your hands off, you sonofabitch!" he shouted.

"I'm trying to protect them," Haviland said, his mouth dry.

The black man, armed with a baseball bat, obviously couldn't hear Haviland over the screaming and shouting. He lifted the bat to swing it. No way to explain to this man, no way to tell him that he was on his side. In the next instant Haviland knew he would very probably be dead unless he acted to protect himself. He drew his gun.

"I'm a police officer!" he shouted.

And then, since this enraged man—this man Haviland had never seen before in his life, this man who had never seen Haviland before—since this man showed no sign of stopping his assault, Haviland fired at his kneecap and brought the man down to the pavement, screaming in pain.

The sound of the gunshot redoubled the violence. The rest of it was a dark red blank to Haviland. He was swarmed over; he used his gun butt as best he could to protect himself. Eventually the uniformed police arrived, almost reluctant, it seemed, to break up the action. Haviland spent hours trying to explain who he was and why he had done what he'd done. Afterward he sought out the man he'd wounded, went to the hospital to see him. He tried to explain that he'd been trying to protect the little girls, had *not* been intent on harming them. The black man lay on his hospital bed, his leg held up by pulleys, his eyes opaque and filled with hate. He didn't believe, couldn't believe, what Haviland was trying to say. Too many years of mistrust and mistreatment couldn't be erased by a few soft words.

So mob violence, the actions of terrorists, sent a

special icy chill through Haviland's blood stream. And now this same unreasoned urge to hurt, perhaps to kill, was growing outside old Pat Mahoney's house.

Haviland was not a praying man, but he heard himself speaking out loud to no one in particular. "Please, find me a way to deal with this thing!"

CHAPTER
EIGHT

The fire on the green had died down from lack of attention. Most of the crowd was now gone, but Haviland could still hear them, the ugly sound of people shouting and jeering. He heard glass shattering.

Once again Teliski's siren split the darkness with its eerie wailing as he and Haviland careened down the street toward Pat Mahoney's house.

Two troopers were there ahead of them, standing with their backs to Pat Mahoney's front door. Some of the crowd had collected burning torches from the fire on the green, and in the wavering light their faces were frightening.

"Come out and tell us where our children are!" someone was shouting.

"Jerry must have told you where he was taking them!"

There was another sound of glass breaking and Haviland saw a young boy, not more than twelve, jumping up and down with delight. He'd scored a bull's-eye.

Haviland and Teliski joined the two troopers at the front door.

"Graninger's around back," one of the men reported. "These people are going to stampede over us any minute. What do we do?"

"Hold your ground," Haviland said.

He tried the front door and found it unlocked. Pat Mahoney hadn't barricaded himself in. Haviland walked in, closing the door behind him.

Old man Mahoney was sitting in the big overstuffed armchair where Haviland had first seen him. He was holding a bloodstained green handkerchief that matched his gaudy tie to the left side of his head. He smiled at Haviland and his blue eyes were unnaturally bright.

"First rock that came through sent a piece of glass right into this thick old head," Pat said. "After that I pulled down the venetian blinds." His smile faded. "I heard about Karl Dickler."

"Bad business," Haviland said. "You all right otherwise?"

"I'm worried about Elizabeth," Pat said.

"Miss Deering?"

Pat nodded. "She went home to the apartment she's got near the bank. Has a cat and dog there to take care of. Worried these crazy people outside might take it into their heads to throw rocks at her, too."

"We'll look out for her," Haviland said. "Where's her apartment?"

"Couple of houses east of the bank." The bright blue eyes clouded. "There's no sign of Jerry anywhere?"

"Or the children," Haviland said.

"It's hard to understand why they're so sure it's Jerry."

"They've got no one else to suspect, Mr. Mahoney. You can understand, they're pretty chewed up out there; the children missing and now Dickler beaten to death. They have to turn on someone. Your son is the only choice they've got, and since they can't locate him, you're the next best thing."

"In the old days I had quite a lot of things thrown at me, but never rocks," the old man said. He chuckled. "That was before I teamed up with Nora Faye. I did a single then—songs, dances, and jokes. Sometimes people didn't think I was George M. Cohan. In the small towns they'd start booing and throwing stuff, like overripe tomatoes and rotten eggs. I think they enjoyed that more than the show. But after I teamed up with Nora I never saw another vegetable or an egg come my way again. She was so damned beautiful, Mr. Haviland, even the roughest drunk wouldn't have thought of throwing anything her way."

"Would you like us to take you somewhere for the rest of the night, Mr. Mahoney? We can't spare the men to guard you here. There's a cot up in one of the offices where I'm located—"

"I don't sleep much these days," Pat said. "Anyway, I don't want to leave here. The first thing Jerry will do when he gets free is call me. He'll know how terribly anxious I am for him. I wouldn't want to miss that call."

"We'll try to break it up outside," Haviland said.

"I can take care of myself," Pat said. "Always had to since Nora went away." He raised his wide blue eyes to Haviland. "Did I tell you about The Great Thurston the last time you were here?"

"Yes, you did, Mr. Mahoney."

"So I did. I remember. I mention it because I

don't think the trick's over, Mr. Haviland. You've only seen the rabbit."

"The rabbit?"

"The Great Thurston used to come out wearing a high silk hat and a black opera cloak lined with scarlet silk. He would take off the hat, make some kind of a pass over it, and pull a big white rabbit out of it by its ears. People would cheer like crazy. Seemed like there was no way that big rabbit could have been in that hat while he had it on, and yet there it was. They'd stamp the house down. Then, cool as you please, Thurston would start taking other things out of that hat—first there'd be a dozen bright-colored scarves, one after the other; then maybe some fruit—an apple, an orange, a melon; then there'd be party stuff, like paper hats, and horns, and those pull-apart party favors. He'd pile all that stuff on the table till it was spilling off on the floor. And then, finally, he'd pull out a little Mexican hairless dog. Each time he pulled something out you'd think it was the end of the trick, but he'd go on and on. It was something you couldn't believe, and yet there it was. You see what I mean about you've only seen the rabbit?"

"No," Haviland said.

"I'll make you a bet, Mr. Haviland—just in a manner of speaking—that what's happened up to now is only the rabbit. I'll bet there's more to come. Much more."

"You think the murder of Karl Dickler is one of those things?" Haviland asked. He sounded grim.

The old man sat silent for a minute, frowning. "Ever seen a good juggler work in vaudeville? Used to be a fellow who called himself Jocko The Magnificent. He could keep six dumbbells in the air, up and down, up and down. But, every once in a while

—not often, but once in a while—he'd drop one. It wasn't meant to happen. I think that's how it was with Karl Dickler. It wasn't meant to happen. But I think the trick will go on because I don't think it's finished. Oh, well, we'll see, Mr. Haviland. We'll see."

The Reverend Mr. John Osgood, Congregational minister in Clayton, eased some of Haviland's tensions for him. He appeared on the front steps of Pat Mahoney's house and berated the crowd, his voice harsh with righteous indignation. They should be home, waiting for their children, praying. Had they no regard for Pat Mahoney's grief? Where the troopers' guns threatened to fail, Mr. Osgood's tongue-lashing did the trick. The crowd began to disperse slowly, a little sheepishly, and head back toward the center of town.

Haviland came out of the house and thanked the minister.

"Righteous anger sometimes leads to strange behavior," Mr. Osgood said. "Those people have a right to be angry. But they have no grounds for abusing Pat. Have they?"

"None—not so far. There is someone else who may need your special kind of help, Mr. Osgood."

"Who?"

"Mrs. Karl Dickler. Oh, I suppose friends are sympathetic, making her a 'nice hot cup of tea.' But she needs another kind of help, something to build her courage. Her husband is dead, her children missing."

"I'll go to her at once," Osgood said. "I was on my way when I heard the nonsense going on down here. Can I tell her anything hopeful?"

"Till we know something definite, hope is all we've got," Haviland said.

Haviland stopped at Joe Gorman's diner. He couldn't remember when he'd last had something to eat. The place was crowded. Everyone wanted to ask questions. He swallowed ham and eggs, toast and coffee too hurriedly to enjoy. Then he elbowed his way out and headed for his office. A grayish dawn was creeping up in the east. Pretty soon there would be enough light for Parker and the troopers to establish an effective search out by the sap house. What was it he'd said to Osgood? Hope was all they had. The children had been missing for nearly forty hours now.

Sheriff Peabody may not have been a very imaginative man, but he was a dogged obeyer of orders. He reported to Haviland that he already had twenty-eight deputies and three troopers checking out the people of Clayton, house to house. Haviland told Peabody to send a man over to keep an eye on Miss Deering's apartment house, and then sought out the cot he'd offered to Pat Mahoney and lay down on it. If he didn't get a little sleep, he thought, he would certainly pass out on his feet. The last thing he was conscious of before a sweet oblivion took over was Pat Mahoney's strange comment that so far they'd only seen the rabbit. . . .

It seemed like only minutes later that someone was shaking him awake. Actually Ronald Peabody had kept him undisturbed for two hours. It was nine o'clock and a bright winter sunlight streamed through the windows of the little office.

"Parker's back with some odds and ends," Peabody said. "Some hot coffee out in the other room."

Haviland struggled up and went to see the FBI

man. Parker was leaning against the steam radiator in the corner, looking half frozen.

"Somebody had cooked hot dogs up there at the sap house," he told Haviland. "We found the cellophane package they came in. Fresh package, bought in the Finast store here in town. We checked there—still trying to check. Maybe seventy-five or a hundred packages of hot dogs bought there yesterday. Seems like the people in this place eat nothing but hot dogs."

"Clerks remember anything?" Haviland asked.

"Checkout clerks don't have reason to remember that kind of sale," Parker said. "They run an order through, ring each item up on the cash register. Hot dogs don't make an impression. Somebody bought caviar, they might recall that. One of my men is still there, trying to tie those franks to someone. Maybe if somebody had bought a lot of them—" Parker shrugged. "We found just one cellophane wrapper, holds eight hot dogs."

"Needle in a haystack," Haviland said.

"We found one other thing that could be helpful," Parker said, "several clear footprints made by a man wearing a rubber-soled boot. A rubber cleat is missing. I got a cast of it, but what do I do with it? Go around like Cinderalla's prince trying to fit a boot to someone?"

"It may come to that," Haviland said.

Trooper Thornton came into the office. He was one of the men involved in Peabody's house-to-house check.

"Stopped by to call my wife, if you don't mind," Thornton said, heading for the phone.

"How is it going?" Peabody asked.

"Nothing that sounds the least interesting," Thornton said, dialing. "Felt like a damn fool going to Nelson Krider's place, but you wanted everyone checked. Ellie? God knows when I'll get home. We're all working around the clock— No, there's no news of the kids." He turned his back, saying something in a low voice.

"Who's Nelson Krider?" Haviland asked Peabody. "Why would he feel foolish going there?"

"Richest man in town," Peabody said. "He's one of the ones who helped get up the ransom. Big ruddy-faced man with white hair. You saw him."

Haviland nodded. He wasn't retaining names by this time.

Thornton came away from the phone. "Krider thought it was a big joke, my checking up on him. His boy Dave was there, and a cousin who's spending the summer—Elliot Krider. They answered questions solemn as you please. Dave has a beaut of a shiner and his face is all scratched up. Took a fall skiing up at the lodge. Well, I'd better get back at it. Waste of time is what I think."

He had just reached the door when Haviland stopped him. "How old are those Krider boys?" he asked.

"Elliot's in college," Thornton said. "Dave's a graduate of State. Why?"

"What's 'the lodge'?" Haviland asked.

"Ski lodge on North Mountain," Peabody said.

"Check out Dave Krider's accident," Haviland said. "People up there would know when and if it happened."

"What do you mean, 'if' it happened?" Thornton asked. "I saw his eye and his face, for God's sake."

Haviland fumbled for a cigarette, his hands not quite steady. "Karl Dickler put up a hell of a fight before they killed him," he said. "There are bound to be some people in this town with Dickler's marks on them."

There was a moment of silence in the room. Then Thornton laughed. "Krider's boy? You have to be crazy, Mr. Haviland."

"I'd be crazy not to check," Haviland said. "You know someone at the ski lodge who could tell us about Dave Krider's fall?"

Peabody knew someone. He put in a call and asked his questions. His face looked strained when he put down the phone.

"Dave Krider hasn't been up there in some time," he said.

"He told you he had a fall at the ski lodge?" Haviland asked Thornton.

"He said 'the lodge.' I don't know of any other."

Haviland stood up. "You got the cast of that rubber-soled boot, Parker?"

"In my car," the FBI man said.

"You agree it might be worthwhile having a talk with Dave Krider?"

"Let's go," Parker said.

"It's just some kind of crazy coincidence," Thornton said. "The Kriders!"

"I gave up believing in coincidences the first year I became a cop," Haviland said. "And that's a long time ago."

Nelson Krider's house was a beautiful white Colonial on a hillside to the south of town, backed by a heavy growth of pine woods. As Haviland drove up toward it with Parker, he felt the blood beginning to tingle in his veins. This was the first real lead they'd had so far. Up to now he had been half dead from frustration.

As they drove up to the front door, they saw

Nelson Krider just about to get into his car. He was a big, hearty man, dressed in country tweeds and a sheepskin-lined topcoat.

"Mr. Haviland," he said. "What brings you here? Any news of the children?"

"Nothing," Haviland said.

"They asking for more money? Because—"

"Nothing like that," Haviland said. "We haven't heard from them since they picked up the ransom from Dickler."

"Poor Karl. Terrible thing," Krider said.

"We came up here looking for your son David," Haviland said.

"Dave? What do you want with him?"

"We think he might answer some questions for us," Parker said. He was carrying a bundle under his arm. Wrapped in newspaper was the cast of the rubber boot.

"I understand he had a skiing accident," Haviland said.

Krider laughed. "Banged himself up pretty good. Lucky he didn't break his neck."

"It was at the ski lodge on North Mountain?" Haviland asked.

"Yes. We all go up there quite often. My wife's a pretty good skier, too."

"Were you with him when he had his fall?"

"No. That was yesterday. I stayed pretty close to town in view of what had happened."

"We'd like to talk to him," Haviland said.

"Sure," Krider said. "He's around somewhere. Come on in the house. But what's the mystery? What can Dave do for you?"

They walked into the beautifully furnished entrance hall. There were paintings on the wall. Haviland knew a little bit about art; his wife

painted as a hobby. He thought he recognized a
Grant Wood and a Benton and a modern primitive
that might have been a Grandma Moses.

Krider went to the foot of a curving staircase
and shouted up. "Dave? You up there?"

"Yes, Dad."

"Come down a minute, will you."

David Krider came down the stairs, brisk and
smiling. He would have been a handsome boy
without the large shiner and the claw marks on his
cheek.

"This is Mr. Haviland, who's in charge of the
kidnapping case," Krider told his son. "And Mr.
Parker of the FBI."

"Hi," the boy said.

"Look like you've been in a meat grinder," Haviland said, trying a smile. His mouth felt stiff.

"Got my skis crossed coming down a steep slope,"
Dave Krider said.

"Yesterday?"

"Yeah. Lucky I wasn't worse hurt."

"That was at the ski lodge on North Mountain?
Your father told us."

"Yes, that's where it was."

The boy was wearing blue sharkskin ski pants,
tucked into heavy boots—rubber-soled—and a
plaid shirt under a leather jacket.

"You weren't at the ski lodge yesterday," Haviland said. "We checked."

"Say, what is this?" Nelson Krider asked.

"You mind taking off your right boot, Dave?"
Parker asked.

The boy's smile looked pasted on. "I wish I knew
what the hell this was all about," he said.

"It's about taking off your right boot," Parker
said.

"Now wait a minute, gentlemen, I think we've gone just about as far with this as we will go without understanding what it's all about," Nelson Krider said. "If Dave says he was at the ski lodge yesterday, that's where he was. I don't care who you checked with. And this nonsense about taking off his right boot. What the hell is that all about?"

Parker unwrapped his package and produced the plaster cast. "This is the cast of a footprint found near Karl Dickler's body, Mr. Krider. It was made by a boot that looks like the one your son's wearing. If your son's boot doesn't match, we'll apologize and go away."

"And if the scraps of flesh the coroner will find under Karl Dickler's fingernails don't match your skin, David, we'll apologize again and go away," Haviland said.

The boy was rigid now, the corners of his mouth working.

Nelson Krider's eyes were wide with shock as he stared at his son.

"So will you take off your boot?" Parker asked.

"Take it off, David," Nelson Krider said. "It can't match, can it?"

"Of course it can't," Dave said, but lie was all over his voice.

"So take it off!" his father shouted at him.

"I think I'm entitled to a lawyer, aren't I?" Dave asked.

"I imagine your future is going to be full of lawyers," Haviland said.

"I guess he goes down to the trooper barracks, Mr. Krider," Parker said. "We'll take his boot off there, whether he likes it or not."

"Wait a minute," Haviland said. "Where are the children?"

"Oh, my God!" Nelson Krider said, in a hoarse whisper.

The boy stood still and silent.

"The ball game is over, boy," Haviland said. "You and your friends will be charged with kidnapping and murder. There is no way in God's world out for you. The children aren't any use to you anymore. Tell us where they are."

The boy didn't move, didn't speak. His eyes were narrowed slits.

"David!" his father cried out.

The boy moistened his lips. "When you fly me out of the country to someplace where there's no extradition, then I'll tell you where the kids are."

"And who your partners are?" Parker said, his voice suddenly shaking with anger.

"When you agree to fly them out with me," David said.

"Along with the money?" Parker's voice rose.

The boy smiled at him. "Of course," he said.

"Where is your nephew, Mr. Krider?" Haviland asked. "His name is Elliot?"

"Oh, God, no!" Nelson Krider said. He'd reached for the back of a chair and was steadying himself.

"Where is he, Mr. Krider?" Haviland repeated.

"He—he went down to the village. He—" The older man couldn't go on.

"May I use your phone?" Haviland asked politely. "We must have him picked up, of course." He moved toward a telephone on a side table and dialed the town clerk's office. While he talked with Peabody and gave instructions, Parker made the arrest.

"Don't you have to read me my rights?" Dave Krider asked.

"In my book it's unfortunate that you have any

rights," Parker said. And then he mumbled, by rote, the necessary words. "Now turn around, put your hands against the wall, and spread your legs."

"Don't!" Nelson Krider whispered.

"Your little boy might just decide to pull a gun on me," Parker said. He slapped Dave Krider's clothes open, not gently. "On your bicycle, buster," he said.

CHAPTER NINE

You could say, in a way, that the case was over. Haviland was sitting in the back seat of Parker's car. Dave Krider, handcuffed, was riding up front with Parker. The boy had confessed. All that was left was to identify his partners in the crime. Almost certainly his cousin, Elliot, was one of them. There was probably another.

Before they had left the Krider house a couple of troopers had been summoned to search for the ransom money. Haviland didn't really expect they'd find it there, but the search was necessary. Nelson Krider was left to break the news to his wife and to contact his lawyer to see that whatever could be done for the boys was done.

Haviland wasn't thinking about the money. Dave Krider was a cool young thug. He held a buried ace and he knew it. The children. In a few minutes, when the news leaked, the whole town would be swarming around the red brick trooper barracks. Do what he asks! Take him to Mexico or

Timbuktu, as long as he tells us where our kids are!

Could they count on his telling them about the children when he was safe? Would they turn him and his brother loose and be left holding the bag, egg on their faces? Suppose they submitted to what was a cool attempt at blackmail? What possible guarantees did they have? None. Haviland had seen criminals at work before. The contemptuous way Dave Krider had reacted reminded him of other moments in a world grown sick with violence. There was no compassion buried in this boy. He wouldn't give a damn for those children, or their parents, or Jerry Mahoney. Twenty years of genteel upbringing counted for nothing. He and his cohorts, with half a million dollars, would use their advantage to turn the screws on desperate people until they could walk away free.

Over my dead body, Haviland told himself.

The news had most of the town headed for the barracks, jamming the roads. Pat Mahoney was forgotten. There was something solid now. They had one of the kidnappers.

Parker literally had to force his way with his prisoner through a crowd of people to the barracks' entrance. A woman reached out and grabbed at the handcuffed man, tears streaming down her face.

"Please, for the love of God, tell us where they are!" she cried out. Haviland recognized Irene Isham—her daughter Betsy was one of the missing kids.

Dave Krider gave her the cold, supercilious smile of a man in the driver's seat. Ben Isham, behind his wife in the crowd, lurched forward, reaching for the prisoner.

"I'll kill the sonofabitch!" he shouted.

Friends held him back.

Parker got his man into the barracks with Haviland just behind. The brick walls seemed to shut out the crowd's noise to some extent. A desk officer began taking down the necessary information from the prisoner, who seemed now to be a happy actor in center stage. Haviland went into Sergeant Mason's office.

"We've picked up the cousin," Mason said. "He should be here soon. It's hard to believe. How is Nelson Krider taking it?"

"How would you expect him to take it?"

"Dave won't tell where the kids are?"

"Get him out of the country, along with his pals, and he might," Haviland said.

"No way we can let them go," Mason said.

"Maybe there's no way we can't," Haviland said. He was thinking of Irene Isham's tearstained face.

Elliot Krider was brought in a few minutes later. The younger boy seemed to be very different from Dave, Haviland thought, as he watched the booking at the desk. He had none of Dave's arrogance. He looked frightened. He wore wire-rimmed, slightly tinted, glasses. He looked anxiously around for his cousin, worried, Haviland imagined, about getting his story straight.

"Keep them apart," he said to Mason. "Don't give them a chance to compare notes."

There was a brief council of war between Haviland, Mason, and the county attorney, a young man named Trotter, who already saw his name in headlines.

"No deals," Trotter said. "We make no deals." He had reddish blond hair and intense blue eyes. He would put on quite a show as a prosecutor in the courtroom. "Now, Krider's lawyer is George

Horween. He's already phoned me. If we don't give these boys all their rights, he'll skin us alive. But no deals."

Parker joined them at that moment. "The boot is a perfect match," he said. "It's open and shut."

"So we don't have to make a deal," Trotter said. "We've got Dave Krider cold."

"First step toward a judgeship," Haviland said, giving the young lawyer a wry smile. "You're entitled, you know, to a questioning period with the prisoners. I suggest you take Elliot first. Dave isn't going to crack. He's the tough one, the leader. There's a chance, if Elliot doesn't get together with Dave, that we can pry something out of him."

The interrogation room at the barracks was a square, whitewashed area with barred windows high up at the ceiling level—no way to look out or for anyone to look in. There was a long stretcher table, with several chairs set on either side of it. Haviland knew about the wall microphones, set so that people outside the room could listen in.

Elliot Krider was brought into the room by a trooper. Haviland, Trotter, and Parker were waiting for him. Haviland found it difficult to connect the scholarly-looking young man with heartless violence. Haviland knew fear when he saw it. The boy's eyes darted from face to face, and there was panic in them. He took off his tinted glasses, almost dropping them as he tried to clean them with a handkerchief. The fluorescent lights in the room showed tiny beads of perspiration on Elliot's forehead.

"You understand," Trotter said in a cold voice, "you don't have to answer questions if you choose not to. That's your right."

Elliot nodded, moistening his lips.

"You know that your cousin David has, in effect, confessed to kidnapping the children and killing Karl Dickler."

"I don't know that," Elliot said.

"Then I'm telling you. He tried to make a deal with us, fly him, you and a third man someplace without extradition laws, and he will tell us where the children are."

Elliot's eyes widened. "Dave said that?"

"That's his idea of a deal. You three go free with the money and then, when you're safe, he may tell us where to find the children—if he feels like it."

"Is that what you're going to do?" Elliot asked.

"You have to be kidding," Trotter said. "The one chance you have for less than the death penalty is to give us instantly, now, information that will get the children back safe."

Elliot stared blankly ahead.

Haviland, leaning against the wall in the corner of the room, spoke in a gentle, casual voice. "You ever been lost in the woods, Elliot?"

"Once, when I was a kid," the young man said.

"How old were you?"

"About eight, I guess. I was visiting that summer, too. I've visited every summer that I can remember."

"The kids on that school bus are only a couple of years older than eight," Haviland said. "I bet you were scared."

"Yeah, I—I was pretty scared."

"And cold, I imagine."

"No, it was summer."

Haviland squinted at Elliot through the smoke from his cigarette. "Can you imagine how scared those kids on the bus are?"

Elliot looked down at his hands. They were locked tightly in his lap.

"Out there in the woods, locked up somewhere, barricaded in a cave with your friend standing guard. They must be scared out of their minds. And it isn't summer now."

Elliot seemed fascinated by Haviland's monotone. He stared, eyes unblinking behind his tinted glasses.

"It's damned cold outside," Haviland went on in his quiet voice. "I keep wondering if you've given those kids anything to eat or drink."

Elliot kept staring.

"What happened when you were lost? Did you just walk home?"

Elliot's mouth twitched. "My uncle found me."

"I'll bet he'd been pretty worried. Eight years old and lost in the woods. He must have been glad to see you."

Elliott seemed lost in the memory.

"Can you imagine how the fathers of these kids are feeling about now? Your uncle probably had some idea where to look. They don't. That's probably why Karl Dickler came back after he dropped the money at the sap house. He was desperate with anxiety for his kids. You came out of that fight pretty well. I don't see any marks on you."

Elliot looked down at his hands again.

"You don't strike me as a cruel man," Haviland said. "I think you can feel sympathy for those people. Did you get a good look at them when you came in?"

Elliot's hands were locked so tightly together his knuckles were marble white.

Trotter couldn't hold himself in any longer. "We could turn you loose out there in that crowd—you and your cousin," he said. "They'd tear you to pieces."

"I don't think that would gain us anything," Haviland said, as though he took Trotter seriously. "I'm hoping to persuade Elliot that he's involved in a lost cause. You won't tell us where the children are, Elliot, unless we get you to a safe place, where the law can't touch you. We won't get you to such a place unless we have the children and Jerry Mahoney back. We both lose unless somebody gives. You know, I'm prepared to believe you didn't mean to kill anyone. But Dickler forced your hand. That was unlucky for you—and for him. If he hadn't come back, you'd have the money, you'd have turned the kids loose, and nobody would have dreamed that you were involved. But the breaks were against you and there just isn't any way out of it now. You understand, legally you're guilty of murdering Dickler, even if you never struck a blow. You didn't touch him, did you? It was Dave and that other guy. Who is he, by the way?"

The door to the interrogation room opened. Sergeant Mason came in with a big, dark-haired, ruddy man—George Horween, Nelson Krider's lawyer.

"You don't have to answer any questions, Elliot," he said.

"Not to worry," Trotter said angrily. "He hasn't."

"I'll take him down to my office," Mason said. There were times when the guilty were much better protected than the innocent. The parents, standing out there in the cold, had no rights. They couldn't get justice for themselves. The law would protect Dave Krider and his cousin Elliot while those kids froze or starved to death. Mason could almost hear Horween demanding that the trial be held somewhere else. The boys couldn't get a fair trial in Clayton. Fair trial! Jesus! He took Elliot down the hall.

Horween stayed behind at Haviland's request. The lawyer's lined, jowly face was set in a rock-hard mask.

"I think Mr. Parker will make it clear to you that there is no question about David Krider's guilt," Haviland said. "He was at the scene of the murder, his boot marks prove it. Before the morning is over the lab will show that Karl Dickler had clawed Dave's face. He has even admitted to the kidnapping, offering to free the children if we'll fly him to some safe place. He mentioned his cousin and another man."

"But you can't prove Elliot is involved or who this 'other person' is," Horween said.

"In time," Haviland said. "In time we'll prove Elliot's part in it and we'll put a name to the other person. The problem is we don't have time."

"Oh?"

"The children, for Christ's sake!" Haviland said, his anger surfacing. He took a deep breath to help regain control. "Now, these boys—and I'm guessing the third person is someone of their age and time—are entitled to a defense. The best defense, which I'm sure you can give them, counselor. But I'd like to appeal to you as a decent man and a responsible citizen. Persuade them to tell us where they've hidden the children. Persuade them that there's no way they can make a deal. Persuade them that it has to be now, today, not some other time, when it will be too late."

The lawyer hesitated. "Maybe those people out there will insist on a deal," he said.

"No way!" Trotter said.

Haviland was looking at the door through which

Mason had taken Elliot Krider. "That boy is our best hope," he said. "I find it hard to see how he got sucked into this scheme in the first place. If you appealed to him as a friend, Mr. Horween, he just may crack."

"As his lawyer I can't just hand him over to you," Horween said.

"All I'm asking is that he tell us where the children are. There's some humanity in that boy."

"I don't promise anything," Horween said.

"I'm not asking for promises," Haviland said. "Just a real effort."

The lawyer left the room.

"What now?" Trotter asked.

"You build your case," Haviland said. "I'm going to find the third man."

Haviland couldn't shake the certainty that Elliot Krider, properly approached, could be made to tell them what was so desperately important to the town of Clayton—the whereabouts of the children.

Through a barred window in the hallway of the barracks Haviland looked out at the waiting crowd. They were hoping against hope that any minute someone would miraculously appear and tell them where their children were. They stood, stamping their feet against the cold, waiting for release from their hours of anxiety.

He had to give it one last try.

Haviland went down the hall to the desk sergeant and asked for Lewis Hoag once more.

Hoag appeared after a few minutes, his face red from the cold.

"I need to pick your brains again, Hoag," Haviland said.

"Glad to get indoors for any reason," Hoag said. "Baby, it's cold outside."

There was a coffee machine in the corner and they got paper cups of a bitter-tasting brew. They went into a small office to the left of the main entrance, a room where, usually, friends or relatives of the arrested were asked to wait.

Haviland laid it on the line.

"I'd hate to have to take that news out to those people," Hoag replied. "You can't make two miserable kids tell you what this town has to know."

"Maybe you can help me get to Elliot Krider," Haviland said.

"How?"

"I want to know every blessed thing you know about him. I take it he's Nelson Krider's brother's boy. If we could reach his parents, get them here, they might help."

Hoag shook his head. "Martin Krider has been dead for fifteen years. Died when Elliot was about four years old. Shelly Krider, his mother—" Hoag shrugged. "Wild horses wouldn't bring her to Clayton."

"Not even to help her son?"

"From her point of view she doesn't have a son," Hoag said.

Impatience made Haviland's voice shrill. "Don't beat around the bush, Hoag! What the hell is going on?"

Hoag found another one of his crooked black stogies and lit it. Haviland coughed as the acrid smoke blew his way.

"If we knew the inside stories of all the families around here, the world might seem like a giant cesspool," Hoag said. "There are all those hates, and jealousies, and fears."

"For Christ's sake, get to it, man!"

Hoag nodded. "All right—here goes. But you

won't like it. Martin was Nelson Krider's younger
brother—maybe eight or ten years younger. Nelson
was the bigshot athlete in school, voted most likely
to succeed, big man with the girls, the usual. And
he did succeed in a big way. There was always
money, and Nelson knew how to make money
make more money. He owns the three biggest
farms in the county, along with controlling in-
terest in half a dozen other prosperous businesses.
Martin always trailed behind, the hero-worshipping
younger brother. He was no athlete, he had no
business abilities. He was something they'd never
heard about in Clayton—an artist. He painted
pretty little pictures of the hills and the sky. It
didn't matter much to Nelson that his brother
didn't amount to anything. I think, in a strange
way, it rather pleased him. Compared to Martin, he
showed up as even more of a giant. And there was
enough money for Martin to indulge himself."

Hoag hesitated. "You know, Haviland, there are
no real secrets in a small town. Things go on, and
people know about them, but mostly they're kept
hidden. I tell something I know about you, you'll
tell something you know about me. So neither one
of us talks. But there were things about Nelson
Krider that a lot of people knew and never made
public."

"What kind of things?"

"For starters, that he's a womanizer. He had
married Emily Taylor, of the wealthy Taylor family. That's another way the rich stay rich. Money
marries money. Emily was Nelson's kind of girl,
everyone thought. She was good at sports. She
would golf and ski with him. And she was handsome. She bore him a son, David. They had a perfect marriage—on the surface. But it wasn't

enough for Nelson. Women were essential to his ego, I guess. There was this girl named Shelly Evans, daughter of a quarry worker, at the other end of the social scale from Nelson. She was a beauty, a very sexy dish. Nelson must have seemed like a real romantic figure to her."

"Hold on," Haviland said. "Didn't you say Elliot's mother's name was Shelly?"

"I did. This is the Shelly Evans I'm talking about."

"Nelson's mistress?"

Hoag nodded. "Of course, that makes it sound like Nelson had Shelly set up somewhere. He didn't. He just went to her when he had the time and the need, I guess. She worked as a stenographer in his office. All he had to do was beckon, and she was available. I don't think he contributed a penny to her support. Maybe she got a few gifts here and there—nothing too ostentatious, of course, or people might get ideas.

"One summer Nelson and Emily decided to take a trip to Europe. Young David was just two, and he was left at home with an army of nurses and grandparents. I don't know how it happened, but sometime during that summer Martin met Shelly Evans and they started to date. People said she went out with Martin to spite Nelson, but I don't think so. Martin was a whole other breed of cat, totally different from his brother—gentle, poetic even, you might say. I don't think he had the slightest notion that there had been anything between Shelly and Nelson. He must have turned out to be one hell of a lover himself, but a loving lover, not just a sexual athlete like Nelson.

"Anyway, when Nelson and Emily got back from Europe Martin had news for them. He had married

Shelly Evans two weeks before. My God, I wish I could have seen Nelson's face when he heard that! Martin had stolen a girl from him! Shelly had betrayed him! And he couldn't even scream about it because of Emily. But he kicked Martin out of the house, cut off the money supply. If Martin could get married, then he could stop painting pictures and support his own family. And Martin, in love with his woman, took her away to New York. They both worked until Shelly got pregnant and had to quit. I guess it was pretty hard going. I have a feeling that somewhere along the way Nelson stuck it to Martin, told him about Shelly's past. But I don't think it mattered too much. Martin loved his wife and she loved him. Nothing in the past mattered. So Nelson's attempt at revenge failed. But Nelson isn't the kind to give up, and his chance came four years later when Martin died."

"How?"

Hoag shrugged. "He just died. I don't know the medical history. And there was Shelly, with a four-year-old son to support on a stenographer's salary. She couldn't work and look after the boy. She couldn't afford household help. And so Nelson had his chance. He and Emily, together, swept down on Shelly. The boy was a Krider, wasn't he? They would arrange for his care. He could come here to Clayton for that first summer. They would see to his schooling. It all seemed kind and generous to everyone except Shelly. She must have guessed that Nelson meant to have his revenge, to steal her child. And—well, that's the way it was. Shelly was never invited to Clayton when Elliot was here. God knows what kind of fairy tale Elliot was fed about his parents. But he grew up feeling that he really belonged to Nelson. David was constantly held up to him as the ideal example to follow, but Elliot is basically like his father. He lacks Nelson's and David's cunning and cruelty. For the last ten years he's been at boarding school and college. I don't know if he ever sees his mother. I don't even know what's become of Shelly. But she isn't going to be any help to you now."

"Yeah. No way to get at Elliot through her," Haviland said dully.

"No way," Hoag said.

Haviland took off his glasses and cleaned them with his white linen handkerchief. "I'm going to have one more crack at him just the same," he said.

He walked down the hall to Sergeant Mason's office. The lawyer, Horween, was there with Elliot. Haviland took Horween aside.

"Any luck?" he asked.

Horween appeared to be genuinely torn between obligation to his clients and concern for the missing children. "The boy seems to be in a state of mild shock," he said. "If he'd told me anything that would help you, I'd pass it on. But he hasn't told me anything."

"I'd like to talk to him alone," Haviland said. "I know you're going to object. But let me take him to the interrogation room. You can watch through the glass panel there and listen. He won't know that you're there, but you can interrupt any time you think I'm going too far. If it's hard for you to make up your mind, Mr. Horween, take a look through that window at the people waiting outside."

Horween didn't move. He didn't want to look at the people. "I'll let you play it your way," he said.

Elliot was taken down the hall. The boy's face had an unhealthy grey look to it. He sat by the long table of the interrogation room, his fingers gripping the edge of it as though he needed to hang onto something. His eyes were fixed on Haviland —the enemy.

"Cigarette?" Haviland asked, offering his pack.

"I don't smoke," the boy said.

"Have you any idea what's going on in this town, Elliot?"

A level, unanswering stare.

"All that matters, all that's left for the people in this place, is to find their children. Do you understand that?"

A slow nod.

"You can't save yourself, Elliot, but you can save them further torture. I've taken the trouble to find out something about you, and I find it hard to believe that you will let these people suffer when it can't possibly help you."

No answer.

"Your father was an artist, Elliot. An artist has to care for people, understand what makes them tick. Think what he might advise you to do at this moment."

"I never knew my father—really," Elliot said. "I was four years old when he died."

"But you are like him."

"I hope not," Elliot said. "My father had no loyalties to people who mattered."

"People like your Uncle Nelson?"

"To his family," Elliot said.

It was as if he was repeating a lesson he had learned from a textbook.

"How do you suppose your mother is feeling at this moment? What if she knew of your involvement? Don't you think she—as any mother would —would plead with you to tell the people of Clayton where their children are?"

"My mother doesn't matter to me," Elliot said. "She was—she probably still is—a whore!"

Haviland sat very still. Nelson Krider had done a very thorough job.

"Unlike your father," Haviland said, "you do have loyalties. You're loyal to your uncle and to David. Am I right?"

The boy nodded. "David has told you what he'll do, and under what conditions. He has always stood by me—when I was deserted by my own family—"

"Did you think your father was deserting you when he died? Did your mother desert you when she accepted help from your aunt and uncle?"

"It really doesn't matter what I think, Mr. Haviland. Maybe I feel sorry for the parents of those missing children, but it's up to David to make the decisions. He's always stood by me, and I have to stand by him now."

"God help you, boy," Haviland said.

He knew there was no point in prolonging this.

Almost reluctantly, Haviland walked out of the barracks into the bright sunshine. He had to face people out there, to tell them that they had solved the murder, knowing that, except for Josephine Dickler, that wasn't what mattered to anyone.

"They refuse to tell us anything about the children," Haviland said. He hated to look at the faces in the crowd. Decent people, grief-stricken, whipped by anger and the need for revenge.

"Can't they be made to talk?" Mercer, the International News man, asked.

"Tell me how, Mr. Mercer. We aren't the Russian secret police, you know. We can't torture them. They think they can force us to get them out of the country. Then they may tell us where the children are."

"So get them out!" a strong voice cried out from the edge of the crowd. It was Warren Jennings, the father of two missing black children. "It doesn't matter what happens to them! I'd like to see them skinned alive, but more than that I want my kids back."

There was a murmur of approval from a hundred voices.

"We need another day to make arrangements," Haviland said. "Can the children last that long? And what guarantee do we have that they'll really tell us anything? You want to take that gamble?"

"We have no choice!" Jennings said.

Overhead there was the sound of helicopter engines. They were out again, searching for some sign of the missing school bus.

"What's your next move?" Mercer asked.

"There's a third man," Haviland said. "Who knows, he may be the one to break down and talk."

It was a slim hope, but it was something positive. Back at the town clerk's office Haviland called Jimmy Craven, Jerry Mahoney's friend and boss, and asked him to check in.

Craven seemed relieved, almost cheerful. The town had forgotten about the Mahoneys now.

"There is a third one to catch," Haviland said. "That's where I need your help, Craven."

"Sure, but what can I do?"

"It would take too long for us to question all these people," Haviland said. "Who are David Krider's friends? He didn't pick a stranger to help. It has to be a close friend, someone who runs with him all the time. There can't be more than three or four young men who fit that description. The one

we want must almost certainly have some marks
on him."

"Marks?"

"Karl Dickler fought desperately for his life,"
Haviland said. "He tangled with at least two men.
We know that from the signs of the struggle.
There isn't a mark on Elliot Krider, so this third
man fought along with David. Help us, Craven.
People will talk to you faster than they will to cops.
We're running out of time."

"Do what I can," Craven said.

Once more Haviland sat alone in the office, his
eyes, burning with fatigue, closed. It was easy to
tell the parents what their "best hope" was. What
choice would he make if his daughter were among
the missing children? He had a feeling that, as a
father, he'd react just as Warren Jennings had.
Let them go, take a chance that they'd live up to
their end of the bargain. But as a policeman, untouched by personal involvement, he couldn't go
along with that. It wasn't just the hours of flying
time to get the Kriders and their friend out of the
country. There would have to be negotiations to
take the killers in, allow a plane to land. That could
take days, not hours. Possibly, while they were still
free, David Krider and the others had done something about food and drink for the children. Now
there'd be no one to carry on with that—except the
third man. And would he carry on? Would he risk
going in and out of town?

The danger to the children was greater than
ever.

The search for the third man had seemed complex and difficult. It turned out to be absurdly

simple. Craven was back in Haviland's office in half an hour.

"There seems to be one pretty solid bet," he said. "Fellow named Paul Sanders. He and Dave Krider were like Siamese twins. They drink together, ski and hunt together, chase girls together. I asked half a dozen people who Dave's close friends are, and they all came up with Sanders."

"You know him?"

"Sure. I mean, to say hello. He's always had a reputation as a wild kid. Suspended from high school a couple of times, kicked out of college. He got a local girl in trouble and her parents decided they'd rather have a bastard in the family than Sanders as a son-in-law. He fits the bill."

"You know where he lives?"

"He's got a cabin in the pine woods back of the Krider place. I think he rents it from the Kriders. His own family kicked him out long ago."

"Can you take me to the cabin?"

"Sure."

"So let's go," Haviland said.

There was a small side road leading up through the pine woods. It wasn't necessary to drive through the Kriders' property to get to the expensively built log cabin. There was a bright red sports car parked in front of it, and a wisp of smoke curled out of a stone chimney. Haviland and Craven got out of their car and knocked on the front door. After a moment it was opened by a red-haired young man wearing a plaid mackinaw over a navy blue wool shirt. He had a sharp, alert, somewhat impertinent face.

"Hello, Paul," Craven said.

It was too easy, Haviland thought. Sanders's lower lip was cut and swollen.

"This is Mr. Haviland, in charge of the case in town," Craven said. "You've heard about Dave and Elliot?"

"On the radio," Sanders said. "Wow!"

"It must have been a shock to you," Haviland said. "How did you hurt your lip?"

"Fooling around in the woods. Tripped over something," Sanders said.

"I say you got it fighting with Karl Dickler and killing him," Haviland said, in his quiet voice.

Sanders's face seemed to freeze, but he kept on smiling. "You have to be kidding," he said.

"I'm too tired to kid anybody," Haviland said. "Is that your car?" He was suddenly playing a hunch, an absurdly simple hunch.

"Yeah, sure."

Haviland walked over and looked inside. What he was looking for wasn't there. He turned back to Sanders. "Mind opening the trunk?"

"You're damn right I mind," Sanders said. His anger sounded false. "What's all this crap about my fighting with Karl Dickler?"

"You and Dave Krider, with Elliot standing watch," Haviland said. "Please open the trunk of your car."

"Like hell I will!"

"Look, young man, don't make it difficult, will you? I'm too pooped to take crap. I can arrest you, charge you with suspicion of kidnapping and murder, and open the trunk myself. So be a good boy, and don't make it complicated."

Sanders hesitated a moment, then reached in his pocket and brought out a ring with two keys on it. He tossed them at Haviland. "Help yourself."

As Haviland reached to catch the keys Sanders spun around and bolted for the woods. Off balance, Haviland didn't have a chance, but Jimmy Craven threw a block at Sanders that would have done credit to a professional football linebacker. Both men went down. Before Sanders could scramble to his feet Haviland was on him, punishing him with a powerful arm lock. He reached inside his coat and took out his holstered automatic. He held it out to Craven.

"Know how to use this?"

"Marine Corps," Craven said, reaching for the gun.

"Cover him. If he tries to go anywhere shoot him in the knee. I want him able to talk."

Sanders sat on the ground, rubbing his arm. Haviland walked back to the car, picked up the keys, and opened the trunk.

Absurdly simple. There was a black suitcase sitting neatly inside, a suitcase Haviland had seen before, first when he gave it to Joe Gorman, and later when it was given to Karl Dickler. The ransom money was all there, stacks of tens and twenties.

Case closed—or almost closed, Haviland told himself. He shut the suitcase and carried it to his own car. Then he went back to Sanders, who still sat on the ground nursing his arm.

"We don't have to play games anymore, do we?" Haviland said.

"Am I under arrest?" Sanders asked. "Why don't you read me my rights?"

"I haven't arrested you," Haviland said. "You don't have any rights until you're arrested, boy. So I am going to take you apart, piece by piece, until you tell me what I need to know."

"You know it all, don't you? You've got the money. That's enough to hang me with, isn't it, even if you can't prove I had anything to do with the Dickler business."

"Oh, we'll hang you, or burn you, or put you in an eight-by-eight cell for the rest of your life. But there's something else, boy, and I want it before you ever stand on your feet again. Where are the children?"

Sanders stopped rubbing his arm and stared at Haviland. "How the hell would I know?" he asked.

"Stop playing games!" Haviland said sharply.

"Oh, brother, you really don't know which end is up, do you?" Sanders said. "I don't know where those lousy kids are and neither does Dave and neither does Elliot."

"Dave knows. He promised to tell us if we'd fly the three of you out of the country."

"Good old Dave, always thinking," Sanders said. "I guess I put my foot in it, huh? Were you going to do it?"

"Not a chance," Haviland said. "One more time —where are those kids?"

"I don't have the faintest goddamn idea," Sanders said. "Come on, wake up, Haviland. We didn't kidnap the children. We don't have any idea who did. We just saw a chance to get rich. We demanded ransom money—we supposed the kidnappers would, too. But there was a chance you might believe us, and you did. If that crazy Dickler hadn't come back after he delivered the money, we'd have made it. That was bad luck. We didn't plan any violence. But we couldn't let Dickler go. You see that, don't you?"

Haviland felt a pulse beating at his temple. There was a ring of truth about the story. But if someone else had kidnapped the kids, why hadn't they heard from them? Out of nowhere he thought of that cockeyed statement of Pat Mahoney's. "So far you've only seen the rabbit." But forty-eight hours and no word from the real kidnappers? That was unreal.

"Let's go over this once again," Haviland said, not recognizing the sound of his own voice. "You and the Kriders were sitting around somewhere when you heard the news about the disappearing bus and the children."

"Right here in my cabin," Sanders said. "It was on the radio."

"And you thought you could rip off the parents for ransom money?"

"Not the parents. They didn't have enough bread between them to make it worthwhile. I said that to Dave. He just laughed and said the whole town would chip in. He said his old man would probably be one of the big contributors. He thought that was pretty funny."

So the case wasn't over. Suddenly they were back to square one. They had wasted a day and a half chasing after these miserable bastards with their get-rich-quick scheme. They were no closer to the children than they had been when the bus failed to come through the dugway forty-eight hours ago.

CHAPTER TEN

The townspeople were still milling around the trooper barracks when Haviland and Jimmy Craven brought Sanders in. Sergeant Mason, Trotter, the prosecutor, and Parker, the FBI man, didn't want to believe the story Haviland told them.

First Haviland had to walk out to that crowd and to the press once more.

Mercer had a question before Haviland could open his mouth.

"We understand you've recovered the ransom money."

"It was found in Paul Sanders' car."

"So the case is wrapped up?"

"Not quite," Haviland said. "You see, we no longer believe they kidnapped the children."

The sound from the crowd was like a giant wave breaking on a beach. There was a scattered murmur and then a roar of protest. Haviland explained the way the boys had made use of the situation.

"Why didn't they leave town with the money once they got it?" Mercer asked.

"That would have been a confession of guilt," Haviland said. "They thought all they had to do was sit around and wait for the kidnapping to be solved. No one would ever look their way. A month from now they could leave casually, go anywhere they pleased without arousing suspicion."

"So what now?" Mercer asked.

"We start from scratch," Haviland said.

"While our children are dead or dying!" someone shouted from the crowd. It was Ben Isham, one of the parents.

"Does that take you back to Jerry Mahoney?" Mercer asked.

That was a question Haviland had hoped he wouldn't be asked.

"It takes us back to the beginning," he said.

Mahoney! The name suddenly swept through the crowd like a volley ball bouncing from player to player. Haviland knew what was going through a hundred minds. The law had failed them. The law had screwed up. They were asking themselves a dangerous question. Hadn't they better take it into their own hands?

What could he say? How could he persuade them they weren't equipped to take charge? How could he persuade them that the police were? The law had wasted two days and they were nowhere as far as the children were concerned. Deep concern for Pat Mahoney and Liz Deering settled over Haviland.

He wedged his way to his car, refusing to answer any more questions. He drove for the center of town and stopped in front of Pat Mahoney's house. The old man had taped some cardboard over the broken glass in his window.

Haviland knocked on the front door and got a

hearty call to "Come in!" Pat was sitting in the big armchair in his living room, a large scrapbook in his lap. The poor old bastard was still living in the past, Haviland thought. But he was cheerful. He had on a different suit, a sharply cut tan gabardine with a blue shirt and a gaudy orange necktie.

"Hi there, Mr. Haviland," he said, waving. "I hear it's all over. You got the boys who did it. Have they told you where the children and Jerry are? It didn't come out the way I thought it would, but it's nice to have it done with."

Haviland sat on the arm of the couch. "It isn't all over, Pat," he said, and he laid it on the line for the old man.

As he listened Pat's bright blue eyes seemed to cloud over. "The whole thing was a trick, a phony?"

"With murder mixed in," Haviland said. "I have to tell you, Pat, that the people are starting to think about Jerry again. They're desperate. They have no other place to turn. I think it would be a good idea if you'd let us place you and Miss Deering in protective custody. Where is she, by the way?"

"At the bank where she works, I suppose."

"Will you come with me, Pat? I'll get someone here to protect your property, but if you're not in the house I don't think they'll bother it."

The old man shook his head slowly. "I'm not leaving here, Mr. Haviland," he said. "Jerry might call. I wouldn't want to miss that when it happens."

"This is serious, Pat. The townspeople aren't responsible for what they may do. They've been driven beyond endurance. They're prepared to believe anything, and Jerry is the only tangible lead they've got."

"I've been driven a little bit beyond endurance,

too," Pat said. "Nora's boy is missing, and I should be trying to find him, trying to help him." And then the cloud lifted and he held out the scrapbook to Haviland. "Did I show you this when you were here before?"

Haviland took the scrapbook, feeling helpless. There was a picture of a smiling couple in cowboy suits. And there was a clipping with a headline that read:

MAHONEY & FAYE
BOFFO BUFFALO

Pat and his beloved Nora looked back at Haviland in their jeweled costumes, their six-shooters drawn, pointing straight at the camera. The clipping contained a description of the act, a dance in the dark with only the jewels showing and the six-shooters spouting flame. "Most original number of its kind seen in years," the Buffalo critic had written. "The ever popular Mahoney & Faye have added something to their familiar routines that should please theater audiences from coast to coast. We are not surprised to hear that they have been booked into the Palace in New York."

"That's out of *Variety*, the show business bible," Pat said. "We had it made, except for Nora's sickness. I think I told you she died before we ever got to New York."

"But you had the satisfaction of knowing you had done it," Haviland said, handing back the scrapbook. "I don't have that satisfaction, I haven't done it."

"My act wasn't any good," Pat said.

"And my act isn't any good now," Haviland said. "Help me, Pat."

"Sure, but how?"

"Let me take you and Liz Deering to a place you'll be safe. That'll let me get on with this case without worrying about you two."

Pat shook his head. "I wish I could do that, Mr. Haviland. I really wish I could. But if Jerry should call and I wasn't here to answer, give him help if he asks for it, I'd never forgive myself. And Nora wouldn't forgive me either."

Haviland tried it the hard way. "There's a good chance Jerry will never call you, never be able to ask you for help, unless I can find him. I don't need you on my back while I'm trying to do that."

But Pat had gone away again, a retrospective gleam in his eyes.

"Once in that week in Sioux City when The Great Thurston was on the bill," he said, "a drunk managed to get backstage somehow, and walked right on the stage where Thurston was performing. Thurston had just pulled the rabbit out of the hat and the audience was applauding and cheering. The drunk grabbed that silk hat away from Thurston and felt inside it, turned it upside down, shook it. There was nothing there. Then a couple of stagehands and an usher came out and dragged the drunk offstage." Pat chuckled. "Thurston was as cool as you please. He smiled, and waved to the guy. Then he picked up his silk hat where the drunk had dropped it." Pat's eyes sparkled. "Out came the colored scarves, and the pieces of fruit, and the party favors, and the little Mexican hairless dog. The audience damn near tore the place down." Pat shook his head in childish wonderment. "That drunk improved Thurston's act. Him grabbing the hat, searching in it, shaking it made Thurston's trick all the more impossible."

Once more Haviland had the curious sensation of being mesmerized by the old man. "You have a reason for telling me this, Pat?"

"Oh, just thought it would amuse you, especially now."

"Why, especially now?"

"Aren't you faced with a magic trick, Mr. Haviland? I mean, how did the bus disappear? You found an answer to that?"

"No."

"So that's the rabbit," Pat said, and grinned happily. "Now you've got these three boys who have taken all your attention. That's the drunk who got into the act and seemed to spoil the trick."

Haviland moistened his lips. "And next will come the scarves, and the fruit, and the party favors, and the Mexican hairless?"

Pat clapped his hands, delighted. "Right on, Mr. Haviland. Right on, as the young people say today."

"What form will they take—the scarves and the rest?"

"Oh, you'll have to work that out for yourself," Pat said. He leaned back in his chair, the happiness fading from his florid face. "I appreciate your wanting to protect me, Mr. Haviland, but I can't leave here. This is my home, the storehouse of my memories." He stroked the scrapbook that lay in his lap.

Haviland couldn't drag the old man out by force. He could invent a reason for arresting him, but that would be a violation of the man's rights, danger or not. Something about the old man's obsessive babbling about magic tricks had put hooks into Haviland. Not that it led anywhere, except to a way of thinking about the problem. Maybe that's what the old man, in his crazy way, was trying to hammer into him—a way of thinking about the problem.

Haviland parked his car in front of the bank and went in. Josiah Cardwell, the president, saw him as he came through the glass doors and got up from his desk.

"Mr. Haviland! We've heard the news. How dreadful for Nelson Krider! His own son—"

"There are other parents in this town," Haviland said. "I wonder if I could talk to Miss Deering."

"I sent her across to the hardware store," Cardwell said. "She should be back in a moment. This town is really shaken up, Haviland. Never saw so many mistakes; deposits incorrect, people forgetting to sign checks. Everybody's thinking about one thing. I understand the ransom money is intact."

"I didn't count it. It looked to be all there."

"Well, thank God for that. A lot of people would be hurting if they'd had to make good on it."

"Including you," Haviland said, suddenly angry.

"Quite true," Cardwell said, with a feeble chuckle. "I hope the troopers will get the cash here to the bank where it will be safe."

"I think I'm more concerned with the children, Mr. Cardwell. Will you ask Miss Deering to call me at the town clerk's office?"

"Of course. And thanks for retrieving the money."

"There's nothing to thank me for, Mr. Cardwell. I haven't done the job I came here to do."

Haviland walked across the street to the Simmons Hardware Company. He didn't have to introduce himself to Ed Simmons, the proprietor. By now everyone in Clayton knew who Haviland was.

"Liz left here five minutes ago," Simmons said.

"She's probably back in the bank by now. Boy, you wouldn't believe how I screwed up my deposit. I must have pressed all the wrong buttons on the calculator. Hard to believe about the Krider boys and Paul Sanders."

"Crimes are committed every day for money," Haviland said.

"I suppose, I suppose."

Haviland went back to the bank. Liz Deering hadn't returned.

"Probably took the opportunity to do an errand of her own," Cardwell said. "I'll have her call you, Mr. Haviland."

The town clerk's office was only two city blocks away. Haviland's frustrations, his anger at the money-grubbing Cardwell, his concern for Pat Mahoney's safety were boiling up into a kind of rage he'd never felt before. He insisted that a man be sent to keep an eye on Pat's house. Then he sat down and pulled a surveyor's map of the town of Clayton in front of him. They'd used it the night before when they'd been sending men out to hunt for Karl Dickler's car.

There was the town, and there, on an accompanying map, was the county. Somewhere in the area represented by these finely drawn lines, these meticulously spaced dots, the tiny but perfect printing, were nine children, a school bus, and its driver. Every inch of this territory had been covered by an army of townspeople, troopers, and special deputies. The school bus and the children and Jerry Mahoney were not there. Or were they? There were scores of barns and outbuildings on farms and estates. There were a dozen abandoned quarries, hunters' cabins in the woods, swamplands, and rocky hillsides where the bus couldn't have gone—but might have. It wasn't likely that every single possibility had been covered. Men would use man's fallible judgment in a situation like this. "The bus couldn't go there." So they didn't look there.

A bus that could disappear into thin air could go to places that defied that kind of judgment, Haviland thought. A magic trick! Damn the old man for filling his head with that nonsense. And yet—and yet in this case you had to begin to believe that the impossible was possible.

Haviland bent over the map again. The dugway, represented by a dotted line, was two inches long on the map, two miles in reality. He had driven through it with Trooper Teliski when he'd first arrived in town. He had accepted Teliski's word on it. The bus hadn't gone into the lake. Not a strand of the wire guard rail on the lake side had been marred or broken. The high side was impenetrable.

Haviland had accepted all that. Now he knew that to be thoroughly satisfied he'd have to go over every inch of it himself. He glanced at his watch. Forty minutes had passed and no word from Liz Deering.

He called the bank. Cardwell was fuming. "I can't understand her taking all this time," he said. "We have payrolls to make up today. She has no right to be gone this long."

The bank was in easy walking distance of Pat Mahoney's cottage. It occurred to Haviland that the girl, worried about the old man, had taken the time to check out on him. He looked up the Mahoney number in the phone book and dialed it.

Pat's eager old voice answered on the first ring. "Jerry?"

"I'm sorry, Pat, it's Haviland."

"Oh." The old man's voice lost its vigor.

"I'm trying to locate Miss Deering," Haviland said. "She left the bank on an errand and hasn't come back. I thought perhaps she was at your place, making sure you were all right."

"She's not here," Pat said. "She stopped by on her way to work. Nice girl. Nora's boy would choose a nice girl, you know. But she had no reason to come back here after she'd made me my coffee."

"If she does come, Pat, have her call me at the town clerk's office."

"She won't come here till after she's through at the bank," Pat said. "Payroll day for all the big quarries and businesses in the area. Busiest day of the week. She works late on a Friday."

Haviland realized he had lost track of the day. It could be Friday or Doomsday.

He felt a small, nagging anxiety for Liz Deering, but he couldn't just sit here and wait for the call to come. He had to get at it, do something constructive.

He went out to his car and drove toward the dugway. He was aware that the town wasn't normal. People weren't going quietly about Friday's business, whatever it was. They were huddled together in groups, at one corner and another—ten or fifteen here, a couple of dozen there. It was as if nobody could bear to be alone. People stared at Haviland as he drove by, and he was aware of their hostility. He had failed them. It was unimportant how clever he'd been in trapping the Kriders and Paul Sanders. He hadn't found their children, he hadn't even gotten a smell of the real kidnappers. The hell of it was he felt guilty. After two days Clyde Haviland, best investigator in the state, had come up empty. He didn't have a single lead.

He felt the dugway was his best—his only—bet. The search there had been quick and desperate. There had to be an explanation for what Pat Mahoney called a magic trick. Maybe a careful, foot-by-foot examination of that two-mile stretch would reveal something the original investigation had overlooked.

The lake side of the dugway was the easiest thing to check out. Haviland drove very slowly all the way to the Lakeview end, studying every inch of the wire guard rail. There was no question about the fact that it was intact. The bus had not smashed through it at any point.

When he reached Jake Nugent's gas station at the Lakeview end he stopped his car and sat motionless behind the wheel. He lit a cigarette and stared straight ahead at nothing. Magic trick. Was there some way, quite literally, the bus could have jumped the fence without touching it? He tried to imagine how, mechanically, it could have been done. Headed toward Clayton, the bus would have been on the other side of the road, on the inside, away from the lake. If Jerry Mahoney swerved to avoid something—an oncoming car out of control, a deer making a sudden leap across the road—he would have turned his wheels in, toward the high gravel bank. He wouldn't have been driving at a high speed through the dugway. From all accounts Jerry was an expert driver, a careful driver, aware of his responsibility to his young passengers. Was there any way in the world, skillful as he was, that Jerry Mahoney could have made a heavy station wagon take off into the air and fly over a four-foot wire guard rail? Haviland found himself smiling grimly. Even The Great Thurston couldn't have managed that!

The only answer, if there was one, had to lie on the inner side of the road, guarded by the high gravel bank and the impenetrable woods.

Covering this was slow, tedious business. Haviland drove his car toward Clayton, perhaps fifty yards, stopped, got out, and walked back, studying the soft shoulder of the road for tire marks, any kind of clue at all. He remembered that Karl Dickler had passed the bus somewhere in the dugway, waving at his children. The disappearance hadn't taken place near the Lakeview end, but Haviland covered it all, a yard at a time. There was nothing. No tire marks, no skid marks, nothing in the gravel bank to indicate that the bus had swerved into it at any point. Even though the ground was frozen, the light covering of snow should have made anything unusual easy to read.

Finally Haviland came to the one critical break in an impenetrable stretch, the old road leading up to the abandoned quarry. Here there were tire marks leading into the woods, but he remembered that Teliski had told him he'd tried to drive up in his police car. For about thirty yards brush was freshly broken and Teliski had spun his wheels trying to force his way up, leaving ruts and scattered earth where the car had dug in. But the trooper had been forced to stop after that because young saplings had grown up in the old road. No one could have driven there for years. Teliski had reported no sign of tracks here before he made his own, but he could have been mistaken. Haviland thought the bus could have come this far, the children been unloaded and taken off on foot through the woods. But beyond the point where Teliski's car had stopped there was only one break anywhere in the carpet of snow that covered the ground. Teliski had evidently gone a little way further on foot. Magic again? Was there any way that nine children and Jerry Mahoney and their captors could walk through the snow without leaving footprints?

Not even The Great Thurston. . . .

Haviland walked back down to the road and continued his examination the rest of the way, yard by yard. As he finally came out of the shaded dugway into the bright sunlight of the village, he realized it had taken him a good hour to come up with nothing. It was about noon.

Aching with fatigue, he went back to the town clerk's office. The woman in the front office told him there had been no phone calls.

"Nothing from Liz Deering?"

"No one has called at all, Mr. Haviland."

He had managed to erase his concern for Liz while he examined the dugway. Now it became intense again. He went back into his own office and called the bank. Josiah Cardwell sounded genuinely worried this time.

"I can't understand it, Mr. Haviland. She's simply never come back. All she had to do was go across the street to Simmons Hardware and come back with a corrected deposit. It shouldn't have taken her more than ten minutes. It's not like Elizabeth to take off without a word."

"I should think not," Haviland said.

He called Pat Mahoney. The old man was obviously still sitting by his phone, waiting for Jerry to call. He hadn't seen or heard from Liz.

"You think there's something wrong, Mr. Haviland?"

There was no use adding to the old man's anxieties. Haviland thought something was very wrong, but he said: "She'll turn up with a simple explanation. Anyone bothered you, Pat?"

"No one been near this place," the old man said. "Maybe they've stopped thinking Jerry's involved. How could they think that, anyway?"

Haviland, his nerves strung tight, went out onto the street and walked to the Simmons Hardware Company. A dozen or more men were gathered outside the store. They made way for Haviland but none of them spoke.

Ed Simmons, a tall gray-haired man, was behind his counter by the cash register.

"You know that Liz Deering never went back to the bank with your revised deposit statement?" Haviland asked.

"Yes. Josiah called me, looking for her," Simmons said. "Strange."

"Did you notice where she went when she left here?"

Simmons shook his head. "I supposed she was going right across the street to the bank. There were customers in the store. I had no reason to watch her."

"Not many places have customers today," Haviland said.

Simmons shrugged. "People need things, I guess."

"Who were the customers you had while Liz was here?"

Simmons frowned. "Joe Feldman, I think, and Marty Lewis. I think they were both here when she started back for the bank."

"Where could I find them? They might have seen where she went."

Simmons pointed toward the door. "They're both out there in that crowd."

Haviland walked out onto the street. The group of men stared at him, silent.

"Feldman? Lewis?" he asked.

Feldman was a short, dark little man; Lewis was a big, powerful-looking blond farmer type. Yes, they had been in the store when Liz was there. No, they hadn't seen where she'd gone. They'd had other things on their minds. No reason to watch her, was there?

There was a reason, Haviland thought. Liz was Jerry Mahoney's girl. Where she went and what she did were important. Half the town believed she and old Pat might be in cahoots with Jerry.

There had been people all over the main street, Haviland thought. If Liz didn't go back to the bank where she belonged, where everyone in Clayton knew she belonged, someone must have noticed.

Haviland went back to his office and called Mason at the trooper barracks. He told the Sergeant about the disappearance.

"I think I'd better have some help down here," he said.

"You think something could have happened to her?"

"I don't know what the hell I think," Haviland said. "She's gone and she shouldn't be gone. With this town in its present mood—"

"I'll send Teliski and Thornton," Mason said. "Ten minutes."

Haviland wandered along the street, stopping to speak to the little cluster of people. Had anyone seen Liz Deering? Some of the people were sullen, some quite willing to cooperate, but the result was the same. No one had seen Liz, not at the time that concerned the detective. A woman had seen her come out of Pat Mahoney's house early in the morning.

"It was about eight-thirty and she started walking toward the bank. To go to work, I imagine."

One of the secretaries in the bank had a desk right by the front windows. She'd seen Liz go into Simmons Hardware.

"It was pretty hairy this morning," the girl said. "It's always rough on payroll Fridays. But today everyone seemed—well, scatterbrained. I heard Mr. Cardwell shouting at Liz to go over to Simmons', and I watched her cross the street."

"Did you see her come out?"

"No. Mr. Cardwell called me just then to take dictation."

Mrs. Anna Murchison had a small boutique and dress shop next to the hardware store. She had seen Liz and actually spoken to her.

"I was standing outside my shop," she told Haviland. "I guess no one was paying much attention to business. I was hoping there'd be some news of those poor children. Liz stopped. I had ordered a dress for her and she was supposed to come in yesterday to try it on. Of course she didn't, not with everything that was going on. 'I can't come in today, either, Mrs. Murchison,' she told me. 'Payroll day and I'll be at the bank till late.' Then she went into Simmons'."

"And when she came out?"

"I don't remember seeing her come out," Mrs. Murchison said. "Maybe I'd gone back in the shop. Maybe somebody had stopped to speak to me."

Troopers Teliski and Thornton arrived. They

brought the suitcase with the ransom money and left it at the bank. They spotted Haviland on the street.

"Liz Deering went into Simmons' place hours ago," said Haviland. "We need to find someone who saw her leave."

In small towns the resident troopers are friends of the inhabitants. They help people in trouble, protect householders from vandalism. People depend on and trust them. They might be hostile to an outsider like Haviland, but Thornton and Teliski were their friends.

After about half an hour Teliski reported back to Haviland. They'd come up with seven or eight more people who'd seen Liz go into Simmons' store, but no one who'd seen her come out.

Teliski chuckled. "There's an old lady, Mrs. Cobb, who lives in that white clapboard house next to the bank. She sits in her window all day long watching people. Her one joy in life. 'I saw her go in,' she says, 'and I didn't see her come out because she didn't come out!'"

Haviland didn't laugh. "Tell me about Ed Simmons," he said.

"What about him?"

"Anything you can think of," Haviland said.

"Well, this is a rough time for him," Teliski said. He's Josephine Dickler's brother, Karl Dickler's brother-in-law. I guess he's worried sick about what this is doing to Josephine—her husband dead, her children lost. Solid citizen. Decent guy."

The corner of Haviland's mouth twitched. "Keep trying to find someone who saw Liz leave the hardware store."

Haviland stood looking across the street at the hardware store, its windows decorated with coffee pots, kitchen ware, snow shovels, and tools. He turned his head to look at the white clapboard house where old Mrs. Cobb sat at her window, spying on her neighbors and friends. "I didn't see her come out because she didn't come out!"

Haviland turned his attention back to the store. It was a rambling, two-story building. The windows on the second floor were small, suggesting that it was some kind of storage loft and not any sort of living space.

Haviland loosened his jacket and walked across the street. The little group of men outside, including Feldman and Lewis, gave him the same hostile looks, but parted to let him into the store.

Simmons was behind his counter, totaling up some sales slips. There were no customers around.

"You find Liz, Mr. Haviland?"

"I'm still looking for her," Haviland said. "Right now I'm going to look in your back room, if you don't mind."

Simmons seemed to freeze. "But I do mind," he said. "What the hell are you talking about?"

"Nobody saw her leave your store, Mr. Simmons, so I've come to the conclusion that she's still here. Mrs. Cobb, across the way, is quite sure she never came out."

"Nosey old bitch!" Simmons said. "Of course she went out, right after she finished straightening out my deposit slip."

"Then you have no reason to object to my looking in your back room," Haviland said, moving around the end of the counter.

"I do object, by God!" Simmons shouted at him. "You have no right to search this place without a warrant."

Haviland reached inside his jacket and brought

out his holstered automatic. "This is my warrant, Mr. Simmons."

The street door opened and Feldman, Lewis, and the others walked into the store, slowly, menacingly. Haviland, holding his gun on Simmons, reached the back door.

"I advise you not to go in there, Mr. Haviland," Simmons said. "God knows what will happen if you do."

Haviland reached with his left hand for the door and opened it. He backed into the room beyond, still holding his gun on Simmons and the others.

He turned and saw Liz Deering. She was sitting in an armchair, a strip of adhesive tape over her mouth, her wrists and ankles taped to the chair. Across from her in another chair was Josephine Dickler, looking like a New England version of Madame Defarge as she knitted a pair of socks.

Haviland saw that the men who had crowded in after him were armed, one with an axe, one with an iron wrecking bar, one with a bailing hook. He had six shots in his automatic. There were at least fourteen of them including Simmons.

He moved cautiously behind Liz Deering.

"This is going to hurt," he said.

With a thumbnail he pried loose an edge of the tape that covered her mouth and then gave it a quick wrench. There was a little gasp from the girl. Josephine Dickler had thrown down her knitting, and she was standing with her hands pressed against her mouth.

Haviland saw uncertainty in Simmons's eyes and sensed that the others were waiting for some kind of word from him. Haviland found the edge of the tape on Liz's right wrist and got that hand free.

"Try to do for yourself now," he said.

Clyde Haviland's eyes, unblinking behind his glasses, were fixed on Simmons. "Are you going to say something, Mr. Simmons, or do you want me to say it?" When the man didn't speak he went on. "You may think because I'm a policeman and a stranger that I don't have any sympathy for you people and your problem. You may think all this means to me is solving a puzzle and identifying a criminal. Not true. I have a daughter of my own, twelve years old. I understood from the first your anxiety, the torture of the parents of the missing children. The badge I carry doesn't turn me into an unfeeling machine." He glanced at Mrs. Dickler. "Your sister is suffering, Simmons, I know that. I'd understand if all of you went down to the barracks, dragged those three boys out of their cells, and tried to hang them from the nearest tree. I'd understand, I might even sympathize, but I would have to try to stop you."

No one spoke, no one moved. The gun aimed at Simmons was rock steady. There was a faint muttering from the men in the doorway.

"Not you or anyone else is going to spoil our chances for getting those children back unharmed," Simmons said. But he sounded uncertain, shaken.

"I'm pretty good with this gun," Haviland said, still very quietly. "It's part of my training. I won't miss anything I shoot at at close range. If you make a move at me, I will kill six of you before you can finish me off. That's quite a price to pay for the uncertain chance that you can use Miss Deering as a bargaining pawn."

"Try to understand, Mr. Haviland," Josephine Dickler said. "We had to have some weapon to use, something to bargain with. We had to!"

"I do understand," Haviland said. "But I can't let it happen."

Liz Deering had gotten herself free and came forward to stand beside Haviland. She put her hand on his arm to steady herself, and he could feel it trembling. But her voice was steady.

"I understand, too, Mrs. Dickler," she said. "If you had told me why you wanted to hold me here I'd have stayed willingly. I'd have stayed because I know you're never going to hear from Jerry. But if it would have made you feel safer—" her fingers tightened on Haviland's arm—"I'll stay here now if it will do any good."

"Oh, my God!" Josephine Dickler said. She turned away crying. The men in the doorway looked at each other.

Haviland looked down at the girl. "Do you want to bring charges against these people?"

"No," she said, shaking her head for emphasis.

Haviland realized he'd been holding his breath and he let it out in a long sigh. He lowered his gun and replaced it in the holster under his left arm.

"I don't suppose there's any reason why we can't walk out of here, is there, Mr. Simmons?" he said.

Simmons looked at the girl. "I'm sorry, Liz," he said. "I guess everyone in Clayton is half crazy about now."

"Let's forget it," Liz said. "I just want to go home."

The group in the doorway parted. Haviland and Liz Deering went through the store and out into the street. She was still clinging to his arm, so tightly he could feel her fingernails through the cloth of his jacket.

"They never told me why," she said, as they walked along together toward the town clerk's office. "They just grabbed me. Until you explained, I had no idea what they wanted."

"Jerry Mahoney's got himself quite a girl," Haviland said.

"They were out of their minds," she said. "God knows I understand that, because I'm nearly there myself. Is there any news at all, Mr. Haviland? Anything? I feel as though I'd been out of the world for days, not two or three hours."

"According to Pat Mahoney, the next thing is that The Great Thurston will start pulling colored scarves out of his hat," Haviland said.

"Poor old darling," Liz said. "He's just as crazy in his own way from his own fear as the rest of them."

"I wonder," Haviland said. "I'm beginning to wonder if he may not be the only person in Clayton who's made any sense so far."

She looked at him, not understanding. He didn't quite understand it himself, but he had a strange feeling that there would be a second magic trick, like the bus, that would be the next step toward—what?

A distant siren, wailing, wobbling, was coming closer. A trooper car was in the dugway, being driven like a bat out of hell toward Clayton. Haviland paused outside the town clerk's office, Liz still holding onto his arm.

It was Sergeant Joseph Mason himself who bought the car, with its blinking top lights, to a screeching stop at the office. His weather-beaten face had taken on a strange gray pallor. He was breathless, like a man exhausted from running. Words came out of him in a kind of choking sob.

"We've found them!" he said. "Or at least we know where they are. Helicopter spotted them."

Just looking at Mason made the small hairs rise on the back of Haviland's neck.

"Where?" he asked.

"The old quarry off the dugway," Mason said. He leaned against his car for support.

"The bus couldn't get up there," Haviland said. "I just checked it out."

"No sign of the bus," Mason said. "But the kids! School books, lunch boxes, a couple of coats—lying on the edge of the quarry. And—and in the quarry."

"In the quarry?"

"Water's sixty-five feet deep there," Mason said. "It's full to within six inches of the top, fed by springs. Clothes floating on the top of the water! Oh, Jesus, Haviland! Do you suppose—?"

CHAPTER
ELEVEN

Mason's news hit the town of Clayton like an exploding hydrogen bomb. People poured out of houses and places of business, running. The groups that had been gathered on Main Street scattered for parked cars. It was less than a mile into the dugway to that old logging road. Within five minutes' time it was obvious that the best chance of getting there was on foot. Two cars had smashed together at the mouth of the dugway, creating a traffic jam like the Sunday night return of weekenders to a big city. People shouted and screamed at each other. Some of them didn't understand the grim details Mason had brought with him. "They've found the children!" was all they knew.

Haviland, rooted to the spot where he'd been standing when Mason brought the news, watched the exodus of the town, scarcely believing what he saw. He had seen something like it before when, as an Army Intelligence officer, he had seen a whole city run for safety in Vietnam. Here, as in that faroff place, there was the roar of overhead motors as helicopters circled and swooped down to treetop levels over the dugway area.

Haviland turned to speak to Liz Deering and found she was gone. She had left him, running with the tide. If the children were in the quarry then Jerry Mahoney might be with them.

The whole thing wasn't possible, Haviland told himself. He had been up that unpassable road an hour ago. There had been no bus tracks, nothing after the first fifty yards except the trail Teliski had made walking a few yards further and coming back. Haviland found himself torn between the need to see for himself and a stubborn refusal to accept the story as fact. The helicopters had been all over the area yesterday and again this morning and no one had seen anything. The old road had been one of the first areas searched in the twilight of the afternoon that the bus had disappeared. There had been no sign of the bus then or an hour ago, when Haviland had covered the ground himself.

And then he saw the light, and he unfroze and headed, running, toward the dugway. The bus had never gone from the dugway up to the quarry. But it could have got there coming from the other side of the small mountain. Haviland knew nothing about the terrain there because no one had mentioned it or thought of anything but the bus disappearing from the dugway itself. But after it had disappeared, it could have gone anywhere in the last forty-eight hours. It could have reached the quarry from a completely opposite direction.

Teliski, in a wailing patrol car, pulled up beside him and threw open the door on the passenger side.

"Come on, let's go!" he shouted at Haviland.

Haviland got in. They drove to the mouth of the dugway and were forced to stop. Teliski worked his screaming siren, cursing at the cars that blocked his way. No one could move. The dugway was dammed up like a plugged drain.

"Have to hoof it," Teliski said.

Even that wasn't easy. They wormed their way between stalled cars, pushing at people who were moving more slowly than they wanted to move.

"Is there a way to the quarry from the other side of the mountain?" Haviland shouted at Teliski.

"Pasture land on the Johnsville side almost to the top," Teliski said, pushing angrily at a woman who cried as she walked. "Only a short stretch of woods to the quarry. They could have brought the bus in that way, I suppose."

The possible was easier to take than the impossible. They came to the old logging road, jammed now with stopped cars.

"Got to get this traffic moving somehow," Teliski said. "We're going to bring in a fire engine and a crane from one of the Lakeview quarries."

"Fire engine?" Haviland asked, puzzled. His mind wasn't working.

"Try to pump out the quarry. The crane has grappling hooks on it in case the bus is down there with the kids. But these cars have got to be moved or there's no way to get 'em up there."

Human ingenuity in crisis is a remarkable thing. Joe Gorman in his four-wheel-drive jeep had been one of the first to arrive on the scene. He had used the powerful little jeep to batter his way to the quarry, handling it almost like a tank, flattening down brush and the few young trees that had grown up in the road. By the time he reached the top there was a trail other cars could follow if the log jam in the dugway could be untangled. Joe Gorman was the first to reach the quarry, the first to see a small red beret floating on the surface of the water. It belonged to his boy, Peter. Joe made a sound like a gored animal and had to be restrained from jumping into the icy water.

By the time Haviland reached the top, there was mass hysteria. School books, lunch boxes, coats, caps, and hats were scattered all over the place. The quarry itself was a giant, gray marble swimming pool. In the days when it had been worked, slabs of the marble had been cut out, going down to a depth of over sixty feet. In those days pumps worked night and day to keep the workings dry against the steady flow of water from mountain springs. When it was abandoned, because new deposits were found more accessible to the railroad and to trucks, it had been allowed to fill, the overflow feeding a noisy brook that led down the mountainside.

Sheriff Peabody had been one of the first to arrive on the scene, wheezing up the hill behind Joe Gorman's jeep. He had managed, unbelievably, to maintain some kind of order. He wanted things left untouched until the fingerprint people from the state police arrived. The books, the lunch boxes, a couple of hockey sticks—all might have prints on them that would lead to the kidnappers. Parents who had arrived hovered over objects they thought belonged to their children.

Some of the younger men, driven by the need for action, discovered a trail leading out through the woods and down over the pasture lands toward Johnsville. A car had come that way, but there was a debate over whether or not the school bus could have come that way too. The tire treads weren't wide enough, some of the men insisted. The children or—and nobody really put it into words—their bodies had been brought here in a different vehicle than the school bus.

Haviland, giving the place a quick, professional survey, realized that there would be nothing left in the way of footprints or tracks of any sort. The place looked as if it had been trampled over by a herd of buffalo.

Sheriff Peabody, sweating from his exertions, was relieved to see Haviland and Mason and a couple of other troopers. For a short time he'd had to handle it all by himself. Mason had begun gathering up things for the fingerprint people. Stunned parents followed him, as if they couldn't bear to let the objects that had belonged to their children out of sight.

Peabody pointed toward the edge of the quarry, where a crowd stood looking down into the cold blue water, motionless, scarcely speaking.

"They just stand there," Peabody said to Haviland. "As if they could will something to come to the surface. Jesus!"

The thought of young bodies in the depths of that freezing water should have been shocking. But Haviland felt nothing. For some reason he couldn't bring himself to believe what he was seeing. Even in this climate of grief and pain he found himself thinking of old Pat Mahoney. What was it Pat had said about The Great Thurston's magic tricks? "The principle is to make your audience think only what you want them to think and see only what you want them to see." The whole damned town was here, the whole damned town saw what someone wanted them to see. The whole damned town believed what someone wanted them to believe.

Why? For what purpose? With what in mind?

Teliski had evidently done his job well, because Haviland heard the clanging bell of a fire engine, urging people out of its way as it lumbered up from the dugway. Haviland looked at the big red pumper and thought that trying to pump out the quarry with that machinery would be like trying to bail out the Atlantic Ocean with a teacup. But the crew received a warm welcome from the crowd. Something was being done at last.

"I don't have much hope for that pumper," Haviland heard Peabody say. "But if we can get that crane up here with its grappling hooks we'll soon begin to bring something up from down there."

"I'd like to talk to the helicopter pilot who spotted this stuff," Haviland said.

"He's on his way," Peabody said. "Probably have to walk from the Lakeview end, the way traffic's jammed up."

Teliski had evidently done a good job with the traffic, though, because Mike Roper, the helicopter pilot, turned up about twenty minutes later. He went into a huddle with Haviland, Mason, and Peabody. He was an Air Force lieutenant, had flown a copter in Vietnam. Tragedy wasn't new to him.

"You spotted this stuff at what time?" Haviland asked.

"Exactly one-ten," Roper said.

"You've been up both days, Lieutenant?"

"Yes."

"So you've flown over this area before?"

"Several times," Roper said. "We were told when we started this operation that these woods back of the dugway were the most likely, maybe the only, place the bus could have got to. Each one of us, when we took off, came to this area first, circled and circled. When we had to go in for refueling or relief, we came back here before we headed in. I covered it four times yesterday and three times today. The last time was when I spotted all that stuff lying around."

"You'd say it wasn't there earlier?"

"Positively."

"There couldn't have been some difference in the light, the glare of the sun, that would have made you miss it?"

"No chance," Roper said. "We criss-crossed it each time so that on one pass or the other we'd be sure to see anything that was important to see."

"Your schedule run about the same each day?"

"Well, not my schedule but *the* schedule. There are four of us. We covered different areas each time up so we wouldn't get bored looking at the same thing and seeing nothing. Because that's just what we've seen until now, nothing."

"And one of you covered this area at about the same time—four times a day?"

"Right. Today was my day."

"What are you getting at?" Mason asked.

"I'm not sure. I wish I knew," Haviland said. "Tell me, Lieutenant, was this schedule exact enough for anyone to guess that a copter would be flying over these woods at about one o'clock?"

"Within ten minutes of that time. Unless, of course, we'd spotted something suspicious and all of us converged on it. But we didn't—haven't. Until I spotted that stuff by the quarry."

"I ask you again, Lieutenant, because it's important. You're sure you couldn't have missed these clothes and books and things on your first two runs today?"

"As sure as I can be of anything in this life," Roper said.

"Another thing, Lieutenant. We think a car brought this stuff and maybe the children from the Johnsville side of the mountain. Did you see anything driving through the fields?"

"I don't remember, but I might have. I wouldn't have paid much attention. Farmers, hunters, sportsmen around. I would have noticed a yellow school bus because that's what I was looking for. I might not have noticed anything else."

Haviland felt a small tremor run over his body as he fumbled for a cigarette and lit it. He'd had this feeling before. He was close to something but he couldn't identify it. He turned to Mason, taking a deep drag on his cigarette.

"If I were to stand up on a tree stump over there and shout to these people that their children aren't in the quarry and they should go home, do you think they'd go?"

"You're kidding," Mason said. "Nobody's going to leave till that crane gets here and scrapes the bottom of the quarry. And, by God, I think it's coming!"

There was the rumbling of a heavy motor and, turning, Haviland saw the giant crane forcing its way up from the dugway. Its long arm reached up into the treetops, smashing branches as it forced its way upward.

"How many people do you imagine are back in town now?" Haviland asked Mason.

"A damn small handful," Mason said. "Girls in the telephone office, a few bedridden invalids and old people who couldn't make the climb. Everything else is shut up tight, you can bet. Couple of troopers manning the barracks. We've got important prisoners there, you know."

The giant crane had moved to the edge of the quarry, its heavy treads blocked by logs of wood. The long arm swung out over the water and the heavy grappling hooks, suspended on steel cables, were lowered, broke the surface of the ice-blue water, and went down to make their grim search.

CHAPTER
TWELVE

There was one person left in Clayton they hadn't thought about. Pat Mahoney was there, in his house with its broken windows. Pat Mahoney was there with his memories and his fears for his son, Nora's boy.

About a quarter to two that afternoon Pat suddenly got frightened. He heard voices, many voices, raised in a kind of hysterical shouting. He went to the front door, opened it, and looked out. He saw people, fifty or sixty people, running toward his house, shouting and yelling. He braced himself. Haviland had been right. They'd all gone crazy in town and they were coming to get him. But the crowd swept by his house without even looking at Pat standing in the doorway.

Bringing up the rear was old Isaac Stanley, trying to keep pace in his wheelchair.

Pat shouted at him. "What's up, Isaac?"

"They've found the children! Up at the old dugway quarry!" And Mr. Stanley continued trying to propel his wheelchair forward.

Now there were cars, driving two abreast down the narrow street like crazy kids trying to race each other. Pat watched the people of the town leave it. He leaned against the door jamb as though his old legs were suddenly too tired to hold him up. If the children had been found in the dugway quarry, then there was the probability that Jerry would be there, too. But Pat made no move to join the exodus. He stood there, listening. The voices had faded away, the speeding car engines were beyond Pat's hearing.

Clayton was suddenly a dead town. Looking down the main street Pat saw that all the stores were closed. The place was unnaturally deserted, quiet with a kind of sinister stillness.

Pat turned and walked slowly back into his house. He sat down in the big armchair and picked up the old scrapbook he'd shown Haviland. He opened it to the familiar place.

MAHONEY & FAYE
BOFFO BUFFALO

He looked at the picture of himself and Nora in their cowboy suits, pointing their guns at the camera. After a moment he closed the book and put it down on the floor again. From the inside pocket of his flashy gabardine suit he took a wallet. It was filled with papers and cards. He was an honorary Elk, honorary police chief of Wichita, Kansas, in 1937, a Friar, a Lamb.

Carefully protected by an isinglass shield were some snapshots. They were faded now, but anyone could see they were pictures of Nora with young Jerry at various stages of his growth. There was Jerry at six months, Jerry at a year, Jerry at

four years. And Nora, smiling gently at her son.
Her love seemed to shine right out of the pictures,
Pat thought.

He replaced the pictures and put the wallet back
in his pocket. He got up from the chair and moved
toward the stairway. People who knew him would
have been surprised. No one had ever seen Pat
when his movements weren't brisk and youthful.
He could still go into a tap routine at the drop of a
hat, and he always gave the impression that he
was on the verge of doing so. Now he moved
slowly, almost painfully—a tired old man with no
need to hide it from anyone.

He climbed to the second floor and turned to the
attic door. He opened it, switched on the lights, and
walked to the area under the eaves. There he
opened the wardrobe trunk where he kept the two
cowboy suits, the Stetson hats, the gun belts, the
boots. For a moment he stood there, stroking one
of the outfits. Nora's things. Then, as though he'd
made a decision, he took his own stuff from the
left side of the trunk—the chaps, the boots, the
vest and shirt, the hat, and the gun belt with two
jeweled six-shooters. Slowly he carried them down
to his bedroom on the second floor.

The walls of that room were covered with photographs of dozens of people "in the business" whom
he had loved and admired over the years, all auto-
graphed. On either side of a full-length mirror
on the closet door were pictures of Nora. When-
ever he dressed, selected a shirt or tie, Nora was
there, approving of his choice, he hoped.

Pat undressed, putting his gabardine suit neatly
on a hanger and hanging it in the closet. Then
he began to dress in his cowboy outfit. He stood
at last in front of the full-length mirror, his cos-

tume complete. The high-heeled boots made him taller than usual. The Stetson was set on his head at a rakish angle. The jeweled chaps and vest glittered in the sunlight from the window. Suddenly old Pat jumped into a flat-footed spread stance, and the guns were out of the holsters, spinning dizzily and then pointed straight at the mirror.

"Get 'em up, you lily-livered rats!" he shouted.

A grim-faced bejeweled gunman stared back at him from the mirror.

Slowly, he turned to the silver-framed picture on his bureau. Nora, a very young girl when the picture had been taken, looked at him with her gentle smile.

"It'll be all right, honey," Pat said to her. "You'll see. It'll be another boffo, honey. Don't you worry about your boy. Don't you ever worry about him while I'm around. You'll see."

Ghost town. That's what Clayton was.

There was no one on the streets. You could hear things you didn't hear otherwise, like the radio next to Mrs. Cobb's window, reporting periodically on events at the quarry. It was feared the children had been drowned—there were reports every ten minutes or so. So far the crane with its grappling hooks had come up with nothing.

The reporters who had inundated the town were nowhere to be seen—all were at the quarry. A streaker, naked as Adam, could have run down Clayton's main street without being noticed by anyone. Every mind and heart was focused on the quarry. Everyone in Clayton was there, in fact or in spirit.

Except for one man.

Pat Mahoney walked down the center of Main

Street, right down the middle of the street, wearing his outlandish cowboy suit. He walked slowly, looking from right to left, staying right on the yellow line that divided the street.

Mrs. Cobb didn't see him because she was crouched over her radio. There was nobody in town so there was no point in looking out the window. She missed what might have been the biggest moment in her life.

The first people to notice Pat's progress were the two girls in the telephone office. They were destined to see it all.

"I'd seen it a hundred times in the movies," Gertrude Naylor, one of the operators, said later. "I guess it was the worst moment of the whole day when I spotted Mr. Mahoney in those crazy clothes, walking down the middle of the street, hands hovering over the guns he was carrying. Just like in the movies, he was, a cowboy walking down the main street of a deserted town, waiting for his enemy to appear, waiting for the shoot-out. His hands floated over those crazy guns, and he kept rubbing his fingers against the tips of his thumbs. I showed him to Millie and we started to laugh. And then, suddenly, it seemed like the most awful thing of all—Jerry Mahoney had murdered those kids and here was his old man, gone nutty as a fruitcake."

Old Pat walked up the steps of the bank. He stopped and turned and looked steadily up and down the deserted street. Then he gave the brim of his Stetson a little downward tug and walked through the glass doors into the bank.

The interior of the bank seemed as quiet as a tomb. Most of the personnel were absent from their posts, probably up at the quarry. Old Mr. Granger, the assistant cashier, had much the same reaction as Gertrude and Millie when he saw the aged, be-jeweled gun toter walk up to his teller's window.

"Good afternoon, Mr. Granger," Pat said, cheer-fully.

Mr. Granger moistened his pale lips. "Good after-noon, Pat."

"You don't seem to be too busy this afternoon."

"N—no," Mr. Granger stammered. The killer's father, dressed up like a kid for the circus. He's ready for a padded cell, Mr. Granger thought.

"Mr. Cardwell not here?" Pat asked.

"No. Most everyone's gone up to the quarry."

Pat turned to look back at the glass entrance doors. Then he asked: "Payrolls been collected yet?"

Mr. Granger glanced at the wall clock. It was 2:30. "No, but they should be any minute."

"Well, while you're waiting I'd like to see a de-tailed statement of my account for the last three months."

Mr. Granger saw Pat lean against the window counter, keeping his eyes fixed on the plate-glass front doors. His hands stayed near his guns and he kept rubbing his fingertips against the balls of his thumbs, just as Gertrude and Millie had seen him do.

"You get a statement each month, Pat," Mr. Granger said.

"Just the same I'd like to see the records for the last three months."

"I had to humor him, I thought," Mr. Granger said later. "So I went back to the vault to get the records out of the files. Well, I was just inside the vault when he spoke again in the most natural way. 'If I were you, Mr. Granger,' he said, 'I'd close that vault door and I'd stay inside, and I'd set off all the alarms I could lay my hands on. You're about to be stuck up, Mr. Granger.'"

Al Granger thought it was part of Pat's craziness. He thought Pat meant *he* was going to stick up the bank. He thought that was why Pat had got dressed up in that cowboy suit and with those guns. Gone back to his childhood, Granger thought. He was scared because he figured Pat was crazy. So he *did* close the vault door, and he *did* set off the alarm. He didn't know then that the alarm didn't go off because he had no way of knowing that the wires to it had been cut on the outside of the bank.

Gertrude and Millie in the telephone office had a box seat for the rest of it. They saw the black sedan draw up outside the bank, and they saw the four men in dark suits and wearing ski masks get out and start up the steps to the bank. Two of them were carrying suitcases and two of them were carrying guns.

Then suddenly the bank doors burst open and an ancient cowboy appeared, hands poised over his guns. He did a curious little jig step that brought him out in a solid, square stance. The four men were so astonished at the sight of him that they seemed to freeze.

"Stick 'em up, you lily-livered rats!" old Pat shouted. The guns were out of the holsters, twirling. Suddenly they belched flame, straight at the bandits.

The four men dove for safety, like men plunging off the deck of a sinking ship. One of them made the corner of the bank building. Two of them made it to the safe side of the car. The fourth, trying to scramble back into the car, was caught in the line of fire.

"I shot over your heads the first time!" Pat shouted. "Move another inch and I'll blow you all to hell!" The guns twirled against and were suddenly aimed steadily at the exposed bandit. "All right, you, come forward and throw your gun down," Pat ordered.

The man obeyed at once. His gun bounded on the pavement a few feet from Pat, and he raised his hands above his head, slowly. Pat inched his way forward toward the discarded gun.

The two men behind the car didn't move. Then Gertrude and Millie, from the telephone office, saw that one of them had gotten around the corner of the bank and was slowly raising his gun and taking a deliberate, two-handed aim at Pat. The girls both screamed. It made old Pat jerk his head around. In that instant there was a roar of gunfire.

Old Pat went down, clutching at his shoulder. But so did the bandit who'd shot him and so did one of the men behind the car. The other two were holding their hands high in surrender. The telephone girls saw the tall figure of Clyde Haviland come around the corner of the hotel next door, a smoking gun in his hand.

Then they saw Liz Deering run across the street to where old Pat lay, blood dripping through the fingers that clutched at his shoulder.

Trooper Teliski's car went racing through the dugway at breakneck speed, siren wailing. His tires made a shrieking sound as he braked and turned up the old quarry road, flattened down now by the passage of Joe Gorman's jeep, the fire engine, and the crane. The trooper's car bounded over stones and old rotting logs. At the top Teliski jumped out of his car and ran toward the quarry, surrounded by people watching the crane lower its grappling hooks for the umpteenth time. So far it had come up with nothing.

"To hell with that!" Teliski shouted. He stumbled as he ran. "Everybody! Everybody, listen!" He was half laughing, half strangling for breath. "Your kids aren't there! They're safe. They're all safe—the kids, Jerry Mahoney, everyone! They aren't there! They'll be home before you will! Your kids—" And then Teliski fell forward on his face, sucking in the damp, loam-scented air.

Twenty minutes later Clayton was a madhouse. People running, people driving, people clinging to the sides of cars and hanging on to bumpers. And as they swarmed into their village they saw, right in the middle of town opposite the bank, a bright yellow station wagon with the school insignia painted on its sides, and children spilling out of it, waving and shouting at their parents, who laughed and wept and reached for them.

From the window of her white clapboard house Mrs. Cobb saw a handsome young Irishman with bright blue eyes take Elizabeth Deering in his arms and hold her in a tight, hungry embrace.

CHAPTER THIRTEEN

Some people didn't care about answers. Their children were safe. Their bank had withstood an attempt to rip off a quarter of a million dollars. Most of them heard that Pat Mahoney had done something to prevent the robbery, but they didn't know anything about the grotesque way in which it had been done. Clyde Haviland, who had failed them earlier, had retrieved his reputation by winning a shoot-out with the robbers and forcing them to tell where the children were hidden.

But the press, headed by Mercer of International News, had to have answers, had to have every detail. They were crowded together outside Pat Mahoney's house, waiting for Haviland, who was inside with Jerry Mahoney and Liz Deering and the doctor who was attending to Pat Mahoney and Sergeant Mason. Haviland didn't have all the answers yet, and he chose not to talk to the press until he did.

The doctor was upstairs with Pat Mahoney, the

first report on the old man being that he had a painful wound but nothing critical.

In the living room with Jerry and Liz and the sergeant Haviland's fingers shook slightly as he lit a cigarette. It had been a long time since he'd been called on to shoot down two men at close range. Gunplay still shook him in spite of his long experience.

"I still don't get it," Jerry Mahoney said. "People thought I had harmed those kids?"

"You don't know what it's been like here," Liz Deering said, clinging tightly to his arm.

Jerry Mahoney turned and saw the cardboard taped over his father's broken front windows, and his face hardened. "Try and tell me, plain and simple, about Pop," he said.

Haviland shook his head, smiling like a man still dazed. "Your pop is an amazing man, Jerry," he said. "His mind works in its own peculiar ways. The disappearance of your bus affected him differently from the rest of us. He saw it as a magic trick, and he thought of it as a magic trick—or rather as *part* of a magic trick. He said it to me and I wouldn't listen—at first. He said it was a magician's job to get you to think what he wants you to think and see what he wants you to see. The disappearance of the bus, the ghastly faking of the children's death at the quarry—it meant one thing to your pop, Jerry. Someone wanted all the people of Clayton to be out of town. Why?

"There was only one good reason that remarkable pop of yours could think of—the area payrolls. Nearly a quarter of a million in cash, and not a soul in town to protect it. Everyone would be looking for the children and all the bandits had to do was walk into the bank and take the money. No cops, no nothing to interfere with them."

"But why didn't Pop tell you his idea?" Jerry asked.

"You still don't know what it was like here," Haviland said. "First people thought you had done something to those kids and that your father and Liz here might be in cahoots with you or know something about it. Then they thought it was the Krider boys and Paul Sanders and you were forgotten. Then when they found out those three had nothing to do with the kidnapping, they turned back to you. No one would have listened to your pop. I only halfway listened to him. Even Liz thought he was touched in the head from worrying about you. He kept throwing me hints, but I didn't buy them at first. Fortunately I didn't forget them."

"So he decided to handle it without help?"

Haviland nodded. "He was, to all intents and purposes, alone in the town. So he went upstairs to the attic, got dressed in those cowboy clothes, and went, calm as you please, to the bank to meet the bandits he knew must be coming. And they came."

"I still don't understand why the cowboy suit?" Sergeant Mason said.

"A strange and wonderful mind," Haviland said, smiling. "He thought the sight of him would be screwy enough to throw them off balance. He thought if he started blasting away with his guns they might panic. They almost did."

"What I don't understand is how, when he fired at them at close range, he never hit anybody," Mason said.

"They were stage guns, prop guns," Haviland said. "They only fire blanks."

"Then he wasn't really armed!" Mason said.

"He thought he could get them to drop their own guns," Haviland said, "and then he'd have a real weapon with which to hold them off. It almost worked, but the one man who'd gotten around the corner of the building got in a clean shot at him. Fortunately I arrived at the same minute and had them all covered from behind."

"How did you happen to be there anyway?" Mason asked.

Haviland laughed. "It was a little like the Chinese water torture," he said. "The old man's hints kept dropping on my head, and dropping on my head, and finally they penetrated. Suddenly I came to the same conclusion. The bank was the target. All the rest of it was magic mumbo jumbo."

"But how did you *come* to that conclusion?"

"With Pat's help, I saw the lunch boxes and clothing in the quarry as colored scarves being pulled out of a magician's hat. Everyone was expected to pay attention only to them, not think about anything else. It was a short step from there to the bank. I just asked myself what there was of value back in the empty, unprotected town. And I remembered that it was payroll day, that there were thousands and thousands of dollars in the bank. Elementary, my dear Watson."

"Damn it, Jerry, I still don't know how they made your bus disappear," Mason said.

"It was simple as pie a la mode," Jerry said. "I was about a half mile into the dugway on the home trip with the kids. We'd just passed Karl Dickler headed the other way when a big trailer truck loomed up ahead of us on the road, blocking the way. A couple of guys were standing around the tail end of it. I had to stop.

"One of them walked over to me, to ask for some kind of help, I thought. Suddenly a gun was stuck in my neck. Another man boarded the bus and covered the kids. They didn't talk much. They just said to do what I was told if I didn't want the kids hurt. Then two other men appeared, opened up the back of the truck, and rolled out a ramp. I was ordered to drive the bus right up into the body of the truck. I might have tried to make a break for it except for the kids. I drove up into the truck, they closed up the rear end of it, and that was that. They drove off, right through the main street of town here."

"Right by the parents who were waiting for their kids!" Mason said.

"An old trick used hundreds of times back in the bootleg days," Haviland said, "and I never thought of it."

"Ten minutes later they pulled into that big deserted barn on the Haskell place. We've been shut up there ever since. They were real decent to the kids—hot dogs, ice cream cones, soda. So we just waited there, not knowing why, but the kids not as scared as you might expect." Jerry laughed. "Oh, we came out of the dugway all right, right through town, but nobody saw us!"

The doctor came down the stairs from the second floor. "You can see your father for a minute now, Jerry," he said. "I had to give him a pretty strong sedative. Dug the bullet out of his shoulder and it hurt a bit. He's pretty sleepy, but he'll do better if he sees you, I think. Don't stay too long, though."

Jerry Mahoney bounded upstairs and into the

bedroom where Pat Mahoney lay, his face very pale, his eyes half closed. Jerry knelt by the bed.

"Pop!" he whispered. "You crazy old galoot!"

Pat opened his eyes. "You okay, Jerry?"

"Okay, Pop."

"And the kids?"

"Fine. Not a hair of their heads touched." Jerry reached out and covered Pat's hand with his. "Now look here, Two-Gun Mahoney—"

The old man grinned at him. "It was a boffo, Jerry. A real boffo."

"It sure was," Jerry said. Then he noticed that Pat was looking past him at the silver-framed photograph on the dresser.

"I told you it would be all right, honey," Pat whispered. "I told you not to worry about your boy while I was around to take care of him." Then he grinned at Jerry, closed his eyes, and he was asleep.

Jerry tiptoed out of the room to find his own girl.

Downstairs Haviland had walked out onto the front steps to satisfy the insatiable appetites of the press.

Printed in the United States
By Bookmasters